Indivisible: With Justice for Some

by

Troy Grice

Your Survival Library

www.PrepperPress.com

Indivisible: With Justice for Some

ISBN 978-0615893044

Printed in the United States of America.

Prepper Press Trade Paperback Edition: October 2013

Prepper Press is an imprint of Kennebec Publishing, LLC

America's day of reckoning has come.

Triggered by a Japanese liquidity crisis, a global run on U.S. Treasuries overwhelms the Federal Reserve and collapses the dollar. Mass inflation sparks civil unrest and panic as store shelves are cleaned out, gas prices rise tenfold, and Americans' life savings are wiped out. Desperate to maintain control, the federal government grows increasingly totalitarian. The president orders the Army home in an attempt to restore law and order, but the Army's battle-hardened attitude and heavy-handed tactics only manage to spur the rebellion on.

The lives of a tormented soldier, a tyrannical sheriff, a vain diplomat and a desperate father converge amidst the chaos of total economic collapse and civil war in contemporary America.

About the Author:

Troy Grice has been a student of economics and a libertarian activist since his twenties. A fan of dystopian novels and science fiction, he describes his own writing as "anti-propaganda" and "counter-myth." He enjoys throwing jabs at both the corrupt establishment and the semi-lucid masses that enable them. For Troy, no manmade institution is beyond reproach. He earned a BA in Economics and has almost twenty years' experience in corporate finance. When not working or agitating for the restoration of the republic, Troy spends time at home with his family in the foothills of Evergreen, Colorado.

To stay notified of the sequels to *Indivisible: With Justice for Some*, sign up for email updates at www.PrepperPress.com.

Chapter 1

They were laughing at her.

Maiden Lane was an Assistant to the Secretary of the Treasury but in addition to that, she was a woman of high-percentile physical attractiveness. A slender, tightly-curved woman of forty five — a glimmering Venus — she illuminated the otherwise murky cosmos of grim bankers.

Ms. Lane had made her sacrifices to the gods of vanity performing self-flagellating penance on hotel elliptical machines at four a.m. almost every morning for nearly twenty years. Her high firm features and smoothly-defined legs were accentuated by a wardrobe of tight-fitting business suits — black, thigh-length business suits.

She often pondered all those women she had passed along the way up career ladder. She pitied those *androgynous trolls*, as she referred to them, mocking how they sheathed their swords of sensuality in scabbards of shaggy uni-brows and general frumpiness. *Losers*, she regarded them.

Maiden, or Mae for short, had no regrets about wielding her aesthetic weapons. *You have to think like a winner in order to win*, she reminded herself in her rare moments of doubt. *Never project weakness. Never go on the defensive. Never pull a punch. A woman must use everything she's got if she wants to reach the capstone. It's a man-eat-man world.*

For Mae, it was easy to titillate and manipulate the depraved, balding, Poindexter-archetype whom she encountered over the course of daily Treasury Department routine. Bankers, diplomats, establishment apparatchiks...they were all shallow careerists who believed in nothing other than accumulating personal prestige. These were colorless, shapeless, ambitious men. Their egos were their drugs and their prescriptions were filled on the stage of geopolitics. The political realm in which they acted was a veritable Hollywood for egomaniacal ugly people.

Mae, the glimmering diva, was much accustomed to being ogled. This ability, in addition to her ruthlessness, got her many promotions. With a flirtatious wink or a juicy pout she could fondle their egos and set them onto her desired course. Maiden's tools served her well — better even than her PhD — as she sauntered up the rungs of the Treasury Department career ladder. Her meticulous hair, hawkish persona, and high-gloss finish polished her impervious shell of armor and ionized her impregnable aura. She was an invulnerable animatron, a sort of robotic, diplomat dominatrix.

...At least up until now.

Ms. Lane was unaccustomed to being mocked.

The two Chinese fellows before her today, sitting across from her in the limo, just weren't into her. This was not an insurmountable barrier for Mae as she could play it straight as well as anyone, but it did implant an irritating stone in her toeless pump. *Perhaps they're gay*, she thought to herself. She closed her knees tightly together.

Mae was sent by her boss, the Treasury secretary whom she referred to as "T", to meet with a high-ranking representative of the People's Bank of China—a Minister Tsang. But no one was there to greet her when she arrived at the Shanghai airport. Mae found this disturbingly unusual. She was, after all, with the U.S. Treasury Department and it was extraordinary to snub U.S. officials. After making a call to the Ambassador's Office and being put on hold for eighteen minutes, Mae was finally instructed to wait outside for a car. She waited with her assistant. Her irritation grew. Three hours passed. Finally, a limousine pulled up.

The white-gloved driver leapt out and in a heavy Mandarin accent asked her if she was indeed "Mae-de-Raine". He was wearing one of those little chauffeur hats tilted to one side and his pants were too short, revealing white socks.

"Maiden Lane," she corrected him annoyingly and with condescending emphasis on the 'L' sound.

The white-gloved driver just nodded with averted eyes, shoved her bag into the trunk and opened her door. It was just as she was about to step in that she noticed the two young Chinese officials inside, each glancing down and fingering their mobile devices.

It was irregular to be met by officials in the car at the actual airport. Mae directed her assistant to take a cab to the hotel rather than ride along as she sensed there might be some unusual negotiations about to take place. Mae didn't want to risk her assistant being called up before some kangaroo senate committee to explain, under oath, what she overheard about whatever unorthodox deal was about to be made in the back of this limousine.

Discretion was the first imperative strategy Mae was taught upon attaining a high-enough degree in the cult of bureaucracy. In Mae's paradigm, a witness creates opportunity for discovery. Discovery leads to transparency. Transparency foments oversight. And oversight is anathema to the efficiency of any bureaucratic system. You cannot be effective as an agency if you have an army of shrill, elected idiots questioning what you're doing all the time. It's best to encourage Congress to snipe away at each other and stay out of the really important matters like economics. Deep down inside, Congress didn't want to know what was *really* happening because then they might actually be held accountable for it.

Ignorance is such bliss, Mae thought.

The two Chinese officials sitting across from Mae were thirty-something and fastidiously dressed in fine black suits and shoes polished to a gleam. Jellied-up black hair, cut into fades, framed their high, wide, Manchurian cheek-bones. Their faces were molded into subtle sneers. Both were still fidgeting their handhelds with eyes hidden behind black sunglasses. Mae nicknamed them Chang and Eng.

"Welcome, Ms. Lane," announced Chang without lifting a glance from his gadget, "How was your flight?" he asked in perfunctory monotone. His English was pristine.

"I suppose I'm a little irritated," Mae answered. "No one was here to pick me up. I had to wait over three hours. I was expecting to meet in person with Minister Tsang at his office at PBC. Are we headed there?"

"Minister Tsang has sent us in his place," answered Eng in similar monotone and without raising his eyes from his gadget.

"We beg your forgiveness, Ms. Lane," continued Chang, "but Mr. Tsang had urgent business with officials in Bhutan."

"I see," Mae continued, perplexed. *Bhutan? What the fuck?* she thought. "Are we going to meet with Mr. Tsang tomorrow, then?" She asked, politely but forcefully.

"I do not think that will be possible, Ms. Lane," answered Chang. "However, we have been empowered by Mr. Tsang to negotiate on the behalf of the PBC."

"You'll have to excuse me but I must say that this is highly unusual. You two gentlemen haven't even introduced yourselves, yet. Do you even know who I am?" Mae asked with condescension and the beginnings of a furrow in her brow.

The two young officials glanced at each other, each aping the other's sneer.

"Of course we do, Ms. Lane," answered Chang. "We are well aware of who *you* are and who *you* represent. You are the assistant to the secretary of the United States Treasury and you've been sent in place of the Treasury secretary to conduct negotiations with the PBC."

3

"Ah," continued Eng, "but the Treasury secretary did not feel it necessary to come to Shanghai to meet Mr. Tsang in person so he sent you in his place. Conversely, Mr. Tsang did not feel it necessary to discuss this matter in person with an *assistant*, so he sent us in his place. So you see, Ms. Lane, there is no need to feel irritated or offended. In fact, Mr. Tsang has already reviewed your latest proposal and we have been instructed by him on how to proceed..."

"...Proceed on behalf of the People of China," completed Chang.

"Forgive me, but what matter in Bhutan could be so urgent as to cause Mr. Tsang to miss a meeting with the U.S. Treasury Department?" Mae snapped.

"I beg your pardon," said Eng. "Bhutan may seem insignificant to the Great Superpower of the Glorious United States of America but Bhutan is China's neighbor and a close and important ally."

Bhutan: a launching point for Tibetan operatives, Mae thought.

"As my colleague indicated, we have been fully empowered to conclude the negotiations here," explained Chang.

"What do you mean by 'here'?" Mae asked, even more bewildered. "'Here' as in here in Shanghai?"

"Uh, more specifically, 'here' as in 'here in this limousine,'" explained Chang.

Mae struggled for a moment to find words, which was an unusual and uncomfortable experience for her. Even when she was trapped, she was always quite nimble at filling in a vacuum with semi-convincing bullshit. She was a politician, after all.

It had to be the uncustomary haughtiness of her Chinese counterparts, she thought. Sometimes the French and the Russians were rude but never the Chinese. The good little Chinese, always so worried about pretense, always so low key and non-confrontational. Mae considered it a cultural inferiority complex. *So why the rudeness today?* She pondered. Mae's irritation was growing into frustration. "So you want to negotiate a swap arrangement that could impact the value of a trillion dollars of your Treasury holdings in the back of a limousine?" Mae stared at them, mouth gaping in astonishment. The Chinese officials grinned. "You're serious? Right here, in this car?" Mae composed herself before continuing. "Fine," she declared. She opened up her briefcase. Fumbling through it, she removed copies of a summary document on glossy Treasury Department letterhead and handed copies of it to both of them. They received their copies with barely extended hands. Their eyes, concealed by their sunglasses, didn't appear to even glance at the pages.

4

"As you can see," Mae explained futilely, "it is a pretty standard reverse-repo—one the likes of which we've executed many times before with the PBC. The bottom line is that we're asking the PBC to purchase $400 Billion using the exchanges. It's the same old drill: work the purchases through your third party dealers so it doesn't set off any market alarms. This should relieve some of the upward pressure on the yuan. You'll then use those dollars to purchase equivalent U.S. Treasuries that will be auctioned over the course of the subsequent seven days. Your purchase will be about half of the seven-day issue. Our Fed will then repurchase those Treasuries from you within the next thirty days...with a *guaranteed* ten percent yield, of course."

The two Chinese officials burst into laughter.

"Guaranteed?" mocked Chang.

They continued laughing.

Mae's frustration turned to anger. *Who in the hell do these stooges think they are?* she thought. "I really think we should be speaking to Mr. Tsang directly about this," she snapped. "This is a negotiation with enormous sovereign ramifications!"

"Like I said before," explained Chang, "we are fully authorized by Mr. Tsang, himself. We have his complete confidence."

Mae knew then that she would get nowhere with these two. She stared at them in disbelief while their laughing trailed off and they went back to fingering their gadgets. She slammed her briefcase shut. She wanted nothing more than to leap out of the limousine, get to her hotel, order a $300 bottle of Chateau Lafite and place some calls to certain contacts who could make these two juniors feel some retributive pain. But that was impossible at the moment as they were now moving forty miles per hour on a congested, twelve-lane highway, motoring through an industrial sector of Shanghai. Even if they were stopped, Mae wouldn't dare get out alone in the middle of Shanghai.

Up until very recent times, the U.S. Treasury was supremely confident in its ability to habitually fuck the Chinese over. The U.S. *owned* China—or so the U.S. banking leadership believed—owned them in the sense that every debtor owns his lender. If the lender squeezes too hard calling in the debt, the debtor might just walk away. The Treasury Department, the biggest debtor in human history knew this and leveraged it. What was China going to do if the U.S. walked away from making its interest payments? Send the United States of America to a collections agency? Send out a Repo-man? Get real. That was the Treasury Department's attitude about it, anyway.

China made the market for U.S. debt since China owned so

much of it. A bad issue, meaning a U.S. debt issue with not enough buyers, would catastrophically drive down the price of China's entire portfolio, ultimately hurting the Chinese the most. Even when the PBC wasn't overtly buying U.S. debt, they were covertly doing it through third party affiliates and through other countries. The U.S. Treasury knew it had China by the short-and-curlies and they could always count on their good little Asian chumps to cough up another half trillion whenever needed, in order to keep the deficit shell game going. The Chinese would never let the Treasury market tank. It would be their own suicide if they did.

This latest negotiation was supposed to be a gimme. Mae was to meet Mr. Tsang like she had fifteen times before. He would initially pretend to be resistant. Mae would flirt, maybe she'd reveal a little cleavage, maybe she'd brush against him as she went through the documents. Then they would ink a deal and go out to dinner. China would then print, or more aptly *keystroke*, a cosmological shitload of yuan, then use those yuan to buy a shitload of dollars, then use those dollars to buy a shitload of U.S. Treasuries. Then the Fed would keystroke a cosmological shitload of new dollars and use those dollars to buy those Treasuries back from the Chinese...plus ten percent, of course. It was Ivy League Genius — a laundering scheme that could be perpetuated ad infinitum. At the end of the day, other than a twenty percent increase in the price of rice, what did the Chinese Commissars have to lose? The yuan would remain soft. Chinese exports would remain cheap. And the Chinese industrial cartels would remain operating at full capacity.

But something was different this time. Mr. Tsang was conspicuously absent. These two juniors were negotiating on his behalf.

Mae hated them now.

Why didn't Mr. Tsang come? she asked herself. *Because of Bhutan? Impossible. No one snubs the United States of America for a Himalayan Deliverance — a tiny mountain fiefdom of Buddhist gong-bangers.* "I just don't understand," she said. "Is this some sort of joke? This entire arrangement today is highly irregular."

"'Highly irregular' indeed, Ms. Lane," remarked Chang.

Mae decided that she especially hated him. She hated his tone. She hated his phony politeness. She hated his Elvis sneer.

"Unbelievable!" She snapped. "You pick me up three hours late in this second-rate limo and treat me like this and... Just take me to Shanghai One so I can speak to someone there."

"We can assure you, Ms. Lane," interjected Eng, "that the PBC will make every attempt to unwind our remaining U.S. Treasury positions in an orderly fashion."

"Yes," affirmed Chang, "in an orderly fashion if that is at all possible."

They both glanced at each other and laughed, again.

"I would not delay in any search for new sovereign buyers," added Eng.

"I didn't follow that," Mae remarked. "What do you mean 'unwind your remaining positions'?"

Chang had to stop laughing and catch his breath before answering. "What we mean is that the PBC will not be entering into any more 'reverse-repos' as you call them. And we want to also inform the Treasury Department that the PBC intends to sell our remaining Treasury holdings — over time, if that is possible."

"What is going on here?"

"You Americans are so arrogant," observed Eng. "The PBC has been quietly divesting itself of treasuries for many months, now. Frankly, we are surprised your forensic accountants have not discovered this."

"We sincerely hope that you are able to find new buyers for your issues. Perhaps Zimbabwe might be interested?" snarked Chang.

Bastards! Mae thought. She reached reflexively for her cell but then thought better of it. *Never show panic,* she advised herself. She composed herself the best she could. "What is happening here?" She asked them. "Don't you understand? Don't you know that this might trigger a meltdown? If you walk away we all lose! Who are you going export your tchotchkes to? Vietnam?"

They laughed again. This time, Eng had to remove his sunglasses and wipe the tears from his eyes. Then he started to preach. "There is an old economics axiom that they used to teach to your MBAs many years ago."

"What are you talking about?" Mae asked.

"We are talking about investment theory, Ms. Lane. You see, China has come to the realization that you can no longer repay us. At least not without printing money in order to do it. America's deficits are now growing so fast that she no longer even has the ability to meet her interest obligations. In other words, your America is bankrupt. America is insolvent and we cannot continue to — — how do you say — —'throw good money after bad.' Yes, that's the term they used at Wharton years ago. The PBC has accepted that axiom and China has

7

decided to cut her losses."

Mae stared at them silently, her brow now deeply furrowed.

"Sunk costs are sunk, Ms. Lane," explained Eng. "The era of China devaluing our yuan in order to enable you fat Americans to watch the Texas Cowboys on 3D televisions made by our workers is over."

"This is outrageous!" Mae barked. "I demand to speak to —"

"Our negotiations are complete," interrupted Chang.

Chang tapped the glass partition and the limousine veered off the highway, coming to a screeching halt at the curb of a bustling intersection. The driver jumped out, adjusted his cap, darted to the trunk in a flash of white socks, and removed Mae's luggage to the curb. He darted around and opened Mae's door.

"Please leave, Ms. Lane. We have no more business with you," Chang.

Mae was frozen in disbelief.

"You may go now!" ordered Chang, who dropped his device as he gestured for Mae to get out. Mae noticed the screen of his mobile was filled with a game of 'Angry Birds'. Chang quickly snatched it up off the floor hoping Mae didn't notice.

Mae crawled out of the limousine. The driver slammed the door shut, shuffled back into the limo and the car disappeared into the smoggy commotion of industrial Shanghai.

Mae darted under an awning, took out her cell phone and speed-dialed her boss, the Treasury secretary. The odors of cooking oil, diesel fuel and dead animal nearly overcame her as it rang. The pheromones of industrialism always made her ill.

"'T' here," came the other end.

"It's Mae. I can barely hear you...I'm out on the street...Yeah, Shanghai...They dumped me here...I don't know what to say...It was a very strange meeting...No, Tsang was not here...He sent two junior guys, real assholes...They rejected it... They said 'sunk costs are sunk'..."

Click.

Mae stared at her phone for a second wondering if she should redial, feeling conspicuous and helpless in her high heels and high gloss and high hemline amidst the noise and smells and dirt of the real world. She backed herself to a wall, looking around for a sign, something coherent, an English phrase, an advertisement, anything American. She couldn't find a single word of anything in English. It was all cuneiform gibberish, everywhere. There was no stamp of the good old USA, not even a Coke machine.

Her terror of conspicuous vulnerability quickly withered into a sense of mere insignificance as the hundreds of people that passed her by every minute paid her no heed. No one cared who she was. A lost American official meant nothing to these Chinese, not even as a peculiarity. They were too busy buying and selling and making a living—producing. These were people of action, oblivious to superficial shock and awe. If Mae were to drop dead at that instant she would just be swept out of the way or stepped over like so much rubbish.

Chapter 2

Specialists Jimmy Marzan and Michael Rollins sat next to each other, packed tightly with four other soldiers into their filthy, rattling Humvee which itself was held together in places with duct tape and bailing wire. They rode in bumpy, dusty discomfort, barely speaking, much as they had done the day before...and the day before that...and the day before that... Marzan and Rollins had been *in country* together for so many months that they had come to the point in their relationship where they had run out of things to talk about—not unlike some old, married couples.

It had been a dull week. The only pleasant aspect of boredom in their dirty, third world ghetto, was the good fortune of unseasonably cool weather. But despite the lull, Marzan and Rollins could feel the omnipresent 'little brown man'—as they referred to him—watching them, grinning at them with his snaggle-toothed grin while covertly plotting their destruction.

Michael Rollins cynically understood this bleak, Goyan world all too well. He enjoyed the life he was leading in it, especially its moral relativism and its ruthless code.

He was a muscular fellow of about five foot ten with blonde hair that was so fair and thin that it blended with the color of his complexion giving him the appearance of baldness. He had had a terrible bout of acne as a teenager which badly pock-marked his face and neck. His grin resembled that of a horse, and his bulging eyes were set too far apart giving him a face that resembled a praying mantis. This potpourri of unfavorable genes made Michael Rollins the subject of ridicule and a reject of the young ladies as an adolescent. From this cold incubator, Rollins matured into an embittered, angry, drifting man-child of twenty six years.

Then Rollins and the Army found each other. Within its ranks Rollins felt, for the first time in his troubled life, acceptance in the form of the embrace of brotherhood that is woven amongst men placed in a milieu of destruction and terror.

Jimmy Marzan, conversely a handsome devil, noticed a fomenting agitation in Rollins over the recent days. He knew Rollins was wound too tightly for boredom and that he had exhausted his venting mechanisms. He was becoming quick-tempered and unpredictable. Just that morning, Marzan noticed when Rollins had discovered that his wristwatch had succumbed to moisture damage and ceased to function. Upon this realization, Rollins calmly removed the watch from his wrist, delicately placed it on the ground, and then hammered it fifteen times into tiny fragments with the heel of his boot.

"Typical Army-issue. Wrecked by water in the middle of a *haji* desert," he complained.

Jimmy Marzan had grown accustomed to Rollin's epithet-laced tirades. He did not encourage them but he did not protest, either. A protest of another soldier's multicultural insensitivity would be classified as an act of overt pussification. The mere anticipation of reprisal would vastly exceed any discomfort associated with enduring the original offense. Jimmy Marzan forced himself to believe that Rollins meant nothing by it.

Colorful language was but one of Rollin's four venting mechanisms, the others being: obsessively manicuring his toenails with his twelve inch Bowie knife, spinning his over-sized, silver, Osiris-eye ring which adorned his right middle finger, and head-banging to his catalog of death metal which sounded more like an M4 fired on full auto than actual music.

The sun was beginning to warm things up. It was going to be a hot day for a change.

Marzan's and Rollins' Humvee was one of a convoy that rumbled down a dusty road. Led by Captain Albert "Al" A. Rick, they blared his musical selection—Elvis—through their PA system, drowning out the morning call to prayer. They eventually came to a stop at a non-descript mud hovel. A dog, some multi-breed mutant, came tearing out of the yard and frothed away at the soldiers drowning out the verse of "...Then one night in desperation, a young man breaks away..." The music shut off and was replaced with the commands of an Army interpreter who was trying to coax the inhabitants out of the house from the safety of his armored vehicle.

The dog was a vile creature. Skinny and covered in a hide of ratlike fur, it barked and foamed and choked itself on its chain trying to lunge at the soldiers. It nearly took a chunk out of the Captain's ankle while he stood next to the road, talking on his radio. No one would be able to get through the gate unscathed with that rabid beast guarding the way.

Rollins took matters into his own hands firing one round at the dog, exploding its left hind paw and sending it into a yelping hysteria. Rollins grinned faintly as he aimed again, but he stopped short of finishing the job.

The man of the house burst out into the yard with his hands flailing, hurling incoherent dialect at a surprised Captain Albert 'Al' A. All rifles aimed at him. Rick, who was not marked as an officer in any manner, drew the frantic man's appeals. Marzan supposed that it was the Captain's aura, if there was such a thing, that had betrayed his rank. The Captain was tall, with weathered skin, and a chin that looked as if it had been pounded into shape in a forge. In addition, all the other soldiers were arranged like spokes, eyes pointing inwards towards him. Despite making himself a target, Captain Rick couldn't avoid looking like the man in charge. Truth was he didn't want to avoid it.

The interpreter was summoned out from the safety of his Humvee and spent about ten minutes describing to the native how it was necessary for the U.S. Army to search his particular mud hovel as there had been reports of a cache of insurgent ammunition stored in his neighborhood. Certainly the native would wish to clear his families' name? In other words, some neighbor had rolled over on him. The native made many assurances as to his innocence in regards to hoarding ammo and RPGs and detonators but did not welcome the soldiers into his home. As a final nudge to get him to comply, Rollins finished off the crippled dog with another rifle shot. The native ended his resistance and led them in.

Five soldiers, including Rollins and Marzan, stormed the well-kept shack and began their room to room search. They pulled a grandfather from his bed and walked him into the common room, setting him down onto a tiled floor in a huddle with three young girls and their mother. Household searches were messy operations and operations that could not be carried out with too much politeness. After three or four searches, even the pretense of restraint was ditched in favor of rapid efficiency. Get in and get out was the procedure.

The soldiers turned the place inside out in just a few minutes. They went through the cupboards throwing food and dishes onto the floor. They went through the bedrooms turning the beds over and yanking the drawers out of their chests. They ripped the laundry from the line dropping it in the dirt, and Rollins dutifully dug his filthy claws through the mother's under things—as if an RPG might possibly be stashed in a lingerie drawer.

With his dog murdered, his children terrified and crying, and his wife screaming, the native man—a father and husband and a proud man as he had a decent house by his countries' standards—sat cowering in a corner of his common room, shielding his face from shame and the bullets that might burst out of the two M4s pointed at his head.

After tearing the house apart and grilling the family for twenty minutes and after not finding any weapons or materiel, the squad extricated itself from the mess. Jimmy Marzan was the last man out and he left the house and the family with an apology, an apology that they could not understand as they spoke not a word of English.

But the U.S. Army did leave, Jimmy reasoned, and they did leave the man with his life and that was worth something. That's how Rollins would process it, Jimmy thought. The *little brown man's* ruined dignity was a small price for him to pay for being permitted to live. The men of the U.S. Army were their liberators, after all.

That was the first of five searches for the 2nd Platoon of Bravo Company and it indeed ended up a very hot day for a change.

Chapter 3

Vaughn's eyes opened in complete darkness. He scanned up and down, left and right into the void trying to orient himself but it took a moment to complete the climb back into consciousness. He finally managed to raise his head up from his pillow and find his clock on the nightstand. The red digital numbers were at first glance incoherent, hieroglyphic nonsense until his lucidity returned.

The time read 3:01.

He reached out next to him feeling the warm curve of Jessica's flannel-covered hip under the duvet. He slid his hand up her side, feeling that she was facing the other way, curled up in a fetal position as she always did when she slept. Her toes were always freezing cold.

"Did you hear that?" he whispered to her.

No reply. She was out. *No need to wake her up*, he thought. He was probably just roused by a dream.

He lay for a few moments staring up blindly into the blackness. He wished that they had a dog — a German Shepherd perhaps — one of those majestic, vicious, and vigilant breeds that would sound alerts at intruders and scare them off, or even better, lock jaws onto their throats.

Vaughn and Jessica Clayton had moved that past spring into an old house in the foothills west of Denver. It was a tri-level on a hillside on a ten acre parcel peppered with ponderosa pine and aspen. A seasonal stream was advertised and it did not disappoint after the late season snows melted off. One of their first mornings in their new home they awoke to find a herd of fifty elk mewing in their yard.

The size of the property appealed to Jess and Vaughn who were recovering suburbanites. They were quickly spoiled by the tranquility and in no time they developed a loathing for the cinderblock strip malls and six-foot privacy fences that hemmed in their prior life.

The lot also had views. What could possibly be said about the views that would do them justice? The panorama, culminating in the snow-capped Mount Evans beat the hell out of staring at a brown, phallus-shaped water tower across the street.

But acclimating to rural life was, in many ways, more difficult than Vaughn had expected. The nights, especially after midnight, were utterly and completely quiet unless the coyotes were yelping. A late-night mountain lion screech was a most unnerving sound as well, unlike anything he had ever heard or expected. But in the absence of those disturbances, the night was a deafening, hypnotic silence that magnified the sense of isolation and intensified all the insignificant and meaningless noises made by a creaking, forty-year-old, plywood house. The wind blowing the bird feeder against the window was the audible equivalent of a car crash in one's driveway. The snapping of a mousetrap sounded like a shotgun blast. The gentle buzz of the refrigerator, inaudible in the daytime, was akin to some roaring machine of heavy industry.

These sounds were meek noises to desensitized, urban dream weavers. The shrieking cop sirens and barking dogs and base-bumping car stereos of the city night drowned out the tinier noises. But out there, on the edge of the wilderness—at least a relative wilderness, anyway—those meek little noises were thunderous sounds.

Vaughn reassured himself that the noise that had awoken him, if it was indeed real and not dreamt, must have been nothing. It was just the old, plywood house shrinking as it cooled in the crisp spring night. *Nothing at all*, he said to himself. *Just go back to sleep.* He adjusted his pillow, positioning his cheek on the cool spot. He closed his eyes. He still wished he had a German shepherd, though.

When Vaughn was a kid, a neighbor boy had a big, vicious, shepherd mix. It barked menacingly at everything, especially anything small and weak and human. The ten-year-old Vaughn, a small and weak child at the time, had to pass that beast on his way to the school bus each morning. Chinook, which was the dog's unfittingly effervescent name, would always be standing sentry at his three-foot chain-link fence between houses, waiting for little towhead Vaughn to pass by. It would glare from behind that meager barrier, one which he could hop with minimal effort, drooling, his dead brown eyes locked onto Vaughn.

The legend of Chinook wove its way through the network of imaginative, neighborhood youths. It was known among these kids, to be a fact and not myth, that Chinook had broken loose one evening from his confines, climbed into an open, second story window, and made off with a neighbor's newborn baby. All childhood legend of course, but a story that resonated with ten-year-olds, especially when one was walking home from a friend's house in the darkness. Many a kid in Vaughn's neighborhood cast anxious glances over their shoulders on such nocturnal journeys.

"Never look behind you cuz you might just see what's gaining."

Vaughn chuckled as he recalled that grammar school advice, given by a chubby neighbor kid who was the chief propagator of the Chinook myth and also one who liked to scare the shit out of the neighbor kids with his Ouija board and black light.

Back to sleep, Vaughn thought. *I'll probably dream of satanic dogs now.*

Vaughn dozed off.

But a sliding noise stirred him again.

Then he heard what sounded like a voice.

Vaughn sprung up. It was definitely a voice. It was a male voice, hushed, whispering, but indeed a male voice. It was not Jessica. She was asleep.

Did I dream it? he asked himself. *Maybe.* He found his clock in the darkness again. It was 3:07. He sat up in bed, his eyes darting around through the black ink of night. He thought about what he should do. *Should I go check it out? I'll have to get up and that'll wake Jess.*

He imagined himself as that ten-year-old, frightened of dogs. *Just listen*, he ordered himself. *Be still.* He put his hand on Jessica again and leaned toward her ear. He brushed away her silken hair and whispered into it. She didn't respond, but her breathing, which generated a faint whistle when she exhaled, became quiet. He knew she was awake.

"Jess..."

"What?" she finally asked in a faint voice.

"Shhh," Vaughn whispered. "Did you hear that?"

"Hear what?"

"Listen..."

They both held still for a minute or so listening to the darkness. A strong breeze combed through the pines outside their window. After a minute, Vaughn decided that it was just the wind. But his eyes scanned the blackness once more just to be sure. Jess was already whistling faintly again, apparently unconcerned. Vaughn gently brushed her hair with his hand and started to lie back.

Crack.

This time Vaughn knew for certain the sound of a footfall on their wood floor. There was absolutely something inside the house. A feeling of terror splashed onto him as if someone had dumped a bucket of ice water on him. He leaned over toward Jessica's ear again.

"I'm going to check on Brooke."

"Okay," she mumbled, barely awake.

Vaughn quietly sat up on the edge of the bed and tried to clear his head asking himself if he was, in fact, awake. *Am I dreaming?* He checked the clock again. It was 3:08. "Should I do this?" he whispered faintly. "Be careful". He fumbled for his glasses on the nightstand being careful not to tip his water glass over. Why was it so difficult to find them in the dark? He groped about until his hand bumped into the lenses. He grabbed them and put them on. He sighed, asking himself again if he was in fact awake.

Creak.

Vaughn's heart began to pound. He was wide awake, now. He reached into the nightstand, and feeling around, he located and removed a small key that he had taped there several weeks before. He removed it. He leaned forward and reached down, feeling along the inside of the bedrail.

"Where is it?" he whispered while groping. "There!" He felt cool steel of the old shotgun. He slid his hand back along the barrel until he felt the wood of the stock. Carefully, he pulled it off the hooks that held it in place on the rail. He had hooked the gun onto the inside of the bed rail with brackets.

Vaughn sat there on the edge of the bed holding the old gun and the key. *I'm sure it's just house noises*, he thought. His heart rate slowed as he listened. Nevertheless, he proceeded. He felt for the lock which looped through the loading and ejection ports. He could not chamber a shell unless it was removed. He pushed the key into the lock considering once more if he should really do it?

Be careful...Oh God be careful.

It was quiet except for the velvety drone of the wind in the evergreens outside. He turned the key. *Keep it pointed down. Keep the safety on. Don't fire unless you know what you're shooting at. Don't even aim it unless you know*, he thought. The cable broke loose and dropped onto the floor. He took a deep breath and stood up with the gun. *Am I being foolish?* he asked himself. *Put it away. This is dangerous.*

Squeal.

Vaughn made his way through the darkness to the door of the bedroom. He quietly cracked it open and looked down the hall, waiting for his eyes to adjust so he could see more detail. The outline of the hallway doors emerged. The glow of a neighbor's porch light, several hundred yards away, beamed though the patio door. Nothing was moving. Nothing appeared out of the ordinary.

Vaughn slipped into the hallway sliding quietly along the wall, shotgun pointed down. He came to Brooke's door. It was partly open which was the way he had left it when he put the toddler down. He gently pushed the door open and went in, using the glow of her nightlight to make his way towards her crib. He listened. There was no sound. He carefully kept the gun pointed away and crept closer to her crib. Still nothing. Closer. He looked into the bed…

There was just enough light to make out the outline of her tiny body. Brooke was on her stomach, knees tucked under, butt sticking straight up in the air, toy monkey to one side. Vaughn could now hear her faint, whistling snore, similar to her mother's. He carefully retreated from the room.

He moved through the hall and down the stairs, guided by the faint blue haze coming from the refrigerator's indicator light. He could make out the shape of the island and the faucet. There was no movement and no sound. He scanned the adjacent dining room and living room. Nothing. No sound.

Then a noise made the hair on his arms stand on end. It was only the refrigerator coming on. He sighed in relief. Everything seemed in order. The living room was dark but quiet. He listened again. No sound other than the purr of the compressor. He started to relax.

Vaughn stepped into the living room and turned toward the office…

…and his heart hammered one enormous beat, the pulse of it he could feel up into his temples. There, in front of him was the silhouette of a man, a man with a small flashlight, silently digging around in his desk. Vaughn wanted to call out but he pulled back ferociously on the reigns of his terror. *Could it be a dream, a lucid dream?* he thought. *No, it's real. He is there. I am awake.*

Vaughn ducked quietly back into the hall, against the wall. He could feel sweat trickling down behind his ears. *What do I do?* He asked himself. He expected paralyzing terror to render him catatonic and helpless but, to his surprise, he didn't freeze up. He was not shutting down with fear, just flush with adrenaline. He thought of his wife, asleep. He thought of his daughter in her crib. His fight-instinct surged in torrents of epinephrine through his arteries and into his muscles. It felt like he could jump twelve feet and knock a man over with a war cry. Waves of tingling pinpricks washed up and down his ribs and legs.

Kill him!
Kill him dead!
Shoot him!
He's in your house. This is your house. He might murder your wife or

you or rape your daughter. Kill him!

Careful, he warned himself. *Easy. Breathe. What if you miss? What if he has a gun? He's cornered. He'll attack. You have to get him with one shot. Get a better angle.*

The adrenaline was pumping so hard he could feel pulsations in his neck. He pushed the safety in on the gun. *Was it on or off? It must be off,* he thought. *Yes, it's off. Easy, now. Get ready to load the shell. Push that little thing in with your thumb. One smooth motion...up, down. Quietly, now.*

Vaughn took another peek around the wall again at the intruder. He couldn't see the sweeping arc of his flashlight anymore. *Where is he?* he asked himself. *He must have heard me. He's got some balls coming in here like this.* He looked again through the living room *Maybe he took off. No. He's trapped in there. I would have heard him. He's got to be in the office.*

Then the intruder poked his head up from behind Vaughn's desk.

Oh shit! Now! Do it now! Vaughn thought. *But what if he shoots back? Oh God. Just do it! Blast him! Pump that shell in and blow his fucking brains out. Reload and keep shooting until you're out.*

Vaughn crept forward carefully, gun aimed into the office at the intruder, hand ready to pump the forestock. He noticed a trickle down his leg. *Pissed myself,* he thought. *Worry about it later.* He crept towards the office, gun aimed through the doorway, aimed towards the intruder's chest.

Shoot now! Shoot! he thought. *What if I miss? You have no choice. This is your house. This is your duty. Protect your family! But I can call the cops! No. They'll never make it in time.*

He tip-toed forward. The intruder was going through Vaughn's desk drawers quickly and silently, flashlight held in his mouth. Closer, Vaughn crept, and closer still, his right thumb on the release, left palm squeezing the forestock, sights aligned, and still closer. Now ready...

He reached the door of the office. *How could he not notice me, now? How can he not hear me?* He poked the barrel of the gun into the office. His body followed. The intruder was still oblivious.
Shit. What now? Vaughn thought. *Shoot him! Do it!*

Vaughn watched him for a moment, wanting desperately to call out. The intruder's head was down as he fumbled around for something under the desk. Vaughn guessed that he wanted to get into the safe. But then the intruder looked up, directly into Vaughn's eyes...

"FREEZE!" Vaughn shouted, reflexively. There was so much

adrenaline coursing through him that his order came out as a high-pitched shriek. "Don't move!" In one fluid motion he slid the forestock back and forward, loading the shell. *Shick shack.* The intruder's eyes darted about looking for an escape but he was trapped. He threw his hands into the air.

"No shoot! No shoot! No shoot!"

"Get your hands up," Vaughn shouted nervously despite the intruder's hands already being up. He stretched them even higher. "Move back!" Vaughn shouted. "Back against the wall!"

"Okay! Okay! No shoot me. No shoot. Okay?"
Vaughn screamed for Jessica. There was no answer. He waited two seconds and screamed again. "Jess!" Then one second more. "Jess!"

"No shoot me, okay? I no move."

"Jess!"

"Is okay. No shoot. I do what you say."

"Get down on the ground!" Vaughn screeched. Then the more commanding quality of his voice returned. "No, just keep your hands up. Jess! God damn it!"

Jess finally appeared, almost running into Vaughn and nearly causing him to set off the shotgun.

"What the hell is your—?" shouted Jess as she switched on the light which illuminated reality in a brilliant supernova.
The intruder came into full view. He was dressed in black sweats and a gray hoodie. He was small, Latino, and tattooed on his face and neck.

"What the hell?" Jess screamed. "Oh my god. What is going on?"

"Call the police," Vaughn ordered.

"No shoot me. Is cool," begged the intruder.

"I said turn around. Shut up! Turn around or I'll blow you away!"

"Okay, okay," he said as he turned around. "Jus hear me. We no have to call cop."

"Shut up," Vaughn replied. "Keep your hands up. If you lower them I'll shoot you dead. Jess, did you call 911?" Jessica was still standing next to him, frozen. "Jess!" Vaughn shouted into her ear. "Call the police! Now!"

Jessica Clayton, the mother, was consumed with other ideas, other instinctual ideas.

"Shoot the bastard!" she ordered.

"No shoot me!" begged the intruder. "Tell lady is okay. No shoot me!"

"Shoot him!" She shouted. "Shoot him, Vaughn. Kill him or I'll kill him myself. I'll go get a knife. You break into my house. Did you come here to take my daughter? Shoot him, Vaughn."

Brooke started crying down the hall.

The intruder looked back over his shoulder. "No shoot me. I make it right. I give you money. No cop. I give you money."

Jess turned for the hallway. "Brooke better be alright or I'll come back here and stab your fucking eyeballs out."

"Brooke's okay," Vaughn assured her. "I checked on her, already. Just call the police. Please." Jess ran to the kitchen. He heard her fumble around in the kitchen junk drawer. "What are you looking for?"

"The phone's dead. I'm looking for the charger."

"You let me go and I give you money. Please," begged the intruder.

"Shut up," said Vaughn.

"I can't find the charger," shouted Jess.

Brooke screamed louder and louder.

Chapter 4

Undersheriff Bob Garrity decided that he liked Neil Diamond which was a divergence from his usual 80s hair-metal playlist. He also decided that he had grown fat since his divorce.

He switched on his interior light and examined his flabby, rose-colored face in the rear view mirror while careening down County Road 73. His chubby cheeks were beginning to squeeze in on the flanks of his push broom mustache and his beady eyes appeared to be receding into his skull. He decided his bloat was a weakness that must be overcome.

No wonder she left you, he muttered to himself as his eyes moved from the mirror back onto the road —

He slammed on the brakes.

His cruiser screeched and fishtailed to a halt in the middle of the road just short of a pair of red, flashing taillights.

It was a moonless night, a pitch black, country night, illuminated only by the range of the headlamps. Garrity turned down the insanely loud whimsical keyboard riff of Diamond's "We're Coming to America" and radioed in. He couldn't see any motion in the car ahead. He flipped on his flashers and siren...still nothing. He aimed the intense beam of his searchlight into the back of the car revealing the backs of two heads.

"Morons," he muttered, while taking mental notes of the details.

Their SUV was new and clean, a Luxury Edition. Its tags were current. The taillights were in working order. It had a "Coexist" sticker affixed to the rear bumper.

Commies! was Garrity's first impression.

Garrity believed he could discern the caste of most civilians by a quick glance at their automobiles. Who says you can't judge a book by its cover? The dangerous ones were the meth-heads with their matted hair and twitchiness. They drove rusty sedans that rode low due to blown out shocks. Another brand of self-manifested self-destruction were the "wiggers," as Garrity referred to them. They were short, skinny, and usually adorned with sparsely grown porno mustaches. Rap music thumped from their spinner-wheeled econo-boxes. It was best to unsnap ones holster when approaching these idiots.

To Garrity, these two flavors were the most dangerous

subspecies of white trash. They all seemingly evolved from the same genetic spawn with their greasy hair, flexed ligaments accentuated with a grease-stained muscle-shirt, short stature embellished by low-sagging pants like the male prostitutes wear in prison. *If they only knew!* he thought.

Both strains of mutant Caucasian had hair-trigger tempers, disrespect for authority, and a foul mouth stuffed full of something to prove. Thankfully, the occupants of the car ahead were neither of these. The bumper sticker indicated something else.

There were other breeds of troublemaker for the undersheriff to worry about as well: "welfare queens" with their dinged up, blue smoke-puffing minivans; drunken cowboys in their diesel pickup trucks; bitchy CEO wives in their German SUVs; punky rich kids in their souped-up rice-burners—they were always on drugs—and don't forget the tree-huggers in their faggoty hybrids—smarmy and passive aggressive, but at least they followed orders.

A clean, luxury edition SUV with a "Coexist" bumper sticker indicated something else, probably an upper-middle-class, metrosexual white male that Garrity could intimidate with a mere snarl.

"They probably hit an elk," Garrity muttered to himself as he approached the driver's side. The window slid down. "Hello," Garrity called out as he approached. There was no answer. "I said HELLO!" He stopped at the rear wheel well of the SUV and took out his flashlight. "Hey buddy, you're endangering me out here! What's your problem? Answer me!"

"Sorry officer," came a timid male voice from inside.

Garrity continued toward the driver's side and shined his flashlight directly into the man's eyes to blind him—Garrity learned that at the academy. He scanned the interior taking mental notation. *Male driver, milquetoast. Shouldn't be any trouble unless he mouths off. Female passenger, crying, probably man's wife. Stereo playing that whiney-ass Dave Matthews...communist affiliation confirmed. Small brat in back seat, sleeping. No signs of drugs. No one looks like they're hiding anything. No odors of pot or alcohol, no wait...sniff...what's that? Wine? Aha! They've been drinking.*

"Do you mind telling me why you're parked in the middle of the highway? You coulda gotten me killed," Garrity asked, switching the flashlight beam into the woman's eyes to blind her, too."

"We hit something," the man explained.

"What did you hit?"

"I don't know."

"Were you planning on taking a look?" asked Garrity.

"It just happened. I wasn't sure what I should do. What if it was just injured? I don't know if it's dangerous."

"Oh, for crying out loud." Garrity's head swiveled toward the front of the SUV and scanned the road ahead illuminated by the headlamps. He couldn't see anything from his vantage. "I want you to stay in your car and keep your hands on the wheel," he ordered the driver. And get her calmed down while I go take a look."

"I don't need any calming down," she said.

Garrity gave her another blast of blinding flashlight into her eyes while he radioed in. Then he walked to the front of the SUV. It was pitch black except for the arc of the lights and the red and blue flashers of his cruiser reflecting off the pines. The road was empty. He swept the darkness with his flashlight as he moved towards the shoulder. Miller moths fluttered and danced in the beams of light.

His flashlight beam swept over a large stone or trunk or — no, it was something else. *How exciting!* he thought. His adrenal glands surged into action. An otherwise dull evening might end on an interesting uptick. He stepped closer. The flashlight's beam locked on. Far away, headlights appeared down the road. *What is it?* he asked himself. It was tan and long, facing into the trees. *Could it be a — yes, yes it's a mountain lion! Oh, what a find. How awesome would this look over my fireplace?"*

Garrity heard the woman grumbling about something back in the car. She had the potential to be a problem for him.

Garrity knelt down over the animal. It didn't appear to be breathing but there wasn't any blood. He unsnapped his holster just in case and leaned in closer, extending his hand. He stroked the fur. It was coarse like straw. The cat didn't move or make a sound.

The car coming down the road approached and Garrity thought it best to walk back to the passenger's side of the SUV. He blinded the driver and the woman again with his flashlight along the way.

"Roll the damn window down, will ya?" Garrity barked at the woman. She complied. "What is she bitching about?" he asked the driver.

The driver tried to hold her hand but she yanked it away.

"Does she have a problem?"

"She's just upset that we hit something."

"That's not why I'm — "

"What did we hit?" interrupted the driver. "Is it dead?"

"It's dead," Garrity answered, with a smirk forming under his mustache.

"So what happens now?" the woman asked.

"Can you calm her down, please?"

"I'm perfectly calm. And you can address me, personally."

"So what was it?" asked the driver.

"It's a cougar."

"Oh, that's terrible," said the driver.

"It is," Garrity answered, as he put his flashlight under his arm and took out his ticket book.

"Are you writing me a ticket?" asked the driver.

"License and registration, please," Garrity replied, as the approaching car whizzed past them in the other lane.

"Are you seriously writing him a ticket?" asked the woman. Garrity scowled, then took the flashlight out of his armpit and blinded her with the beam again. He had a low tolerance for citizens exhibiting contempt-of-cop.

"Please stop shining that light in my eyes," she said.

"I said license and registration!" Garrity growled. "Have you been drinking?"

"No, not at all. Not tonight, officer."

The driver reached into his visor, took out his papers and handed them to Garrity who took them back to his cruiser. Once inside, Garrity keyed in the info and radioed dispatch. Another set of headlights appeared, far off up the road. The driver's papers were in order with no outstanding warrants. Garrity filled out a citation, making notes as to the woman's belligerent attitude. Then he waited an additional thirteen minutes just because he could. He wasn't sure if he wanted to put the driver through the roadside test. It was such a pain in the ass. Two more cars zipped past. To pass the time, he fumbled with his iPod finally settling on "Here I Go Again" by Whitesnake.

He glanced up, startled to find that the driver was getting out of his SUV. Garrity quickly jumped out of the cruiser to subdue him.

"What the hell do you think you're doing?" he shouted at the driver.

"Are you seriously going to write me a ticket?" the man asked.

"That's right. Now get your ass back in your car. You are endangering a sheriff!"

"I want to know why you're writing me a ticket."

"I'm the one with the badge and the gun. I ask the questions and I give the orders. I said get your ass back in your car or I'll tack on a DUI," Garrity hollered as he reached for his holster. "I've had about enough of you two."

"I didn't do anything wrong. I just want—"

"Get your ass back in your car or I will take you down. Do you understand?"

"For what? For asking you a question?"

The woman in the car started to shout. The toddler who was asleep woke up and started to scream. Another set of headlights appeared from up the road.

"This is your last chance," Garrity commanded as he reached down along his belt to his holster.

The woman shouted, "No, no!"

"I have a question. That's all. I just want to know why you are writing me a ticket. It's just a question. Just answer that and I'll get back in my car."

"You will do as I say or I will put you down. Get your ass back in your car!" Garrity could not believe the defiant attitude of this prole. Even the meth-heads, as argumentative as they typically were, had more sense than this idiot. Garrity pondered at what moment he should he draw.

"Come back to the car!" the woman shouted. "You're going to get get run over!"

The headlights from down the road drew closer. The whoosh of its tires on the road grew louder.

"You have no right to give me a ticket for hitting that thing," the driver argued. "There was nothing I could do. It ran out in front of—"

Garrity drew and charged forward, following the beam of his flashlight into the man's face. He fired, dropping the man to the ground in a heap, screaming and writhing in pain from the shock of the taser. The woman shouted obscenities in response. The toddler screamed. The approaching car decelerated with a screech. Garrity pounced onto the man, driving his knee into his back, deftly cuffing him—they taught him how to do that at the police academy, too.

"Why are you doing this?" shouted the man.

"Stop resisting. You're under arrest!" Garrity declared.

"I'm not resisting."

"You—are—under—arrest!"

"For what?"

"For resisting arrest."

"You're arresting me for resisting arrest? What the fuck? That doesn't make sense."

"Shut up or I'll taser you again."

The approaching car came to a stop which added to Garrity's agitation. There were too many variables for him to control, now. He was highly stressed. He yanked the driver up and shoved him into the back of his cruiser.

"Anything we can help with, officer?" asked the driver of the other car.

"It's 'sheriff', not 'officer'. Do I look like a god damn city cop to you? Move along."

Garrity went back to the SUV to subdue the woman who had since exited her vehicle and was now standing on the shoulder of the road cursing him. Garrity drew his gun but the sight of it had no effect on her. She continued insulting him and giving him dehumanizing stares. She looked as if she wanted to rip his eyeballs out with her fingernails — deadly weapons as far as he was concerned. The toddler in the back seat cried. Garrity took aim at her but thought for a moment about the witnesses in the car in the opposite lane which had not yet moved on. He holstered his gun and charged the woman, tackling her down onto the rocky shoulder.

The other car slowly pulled away.

As Garrity knelt on the woman, frisked her, and radioed for backup, the cougar, which was only stunned, gathered herself up and limped back into woods.

Chapter 5

Mae was rescued from the Chinese megalopolis by a driver from the U.S. embassy. She spent two days at the U.S. compound trying to stay out of the way of the manic document shredding and frenzied packing. The morning of the third day, she was hustled onto a helicopter — fall-of-Saigon-style — and choppered to the airport with a number of diplomats. They loaded everything onto a 747 which whisked them away into the Pacific night.

The jumbo jet made one stop at Ted Stevens International Airport in Anchorage where they sat on the tarmac for four hours. A Greyhound bus pulled alongside the plane and another two dozen Treasury officials and diplomats, who had flown in from other Asian capitals, boarded the 747. Several hundred trunks were offloaded by forklifts, stacked onto pallets, and reloaded into a semi-trailer bearing a logo for corn chips. The tractor-trailer drove off the tarmac. It had no final destination.

By nine a.m., they were wheels up, again. Five hours later, they landed at Denver International under a cloudless blue sky. The diplomats and officials deplaned onto the tarmac. A fleet of black, tinted SUVs pulled up. One security agent, dressed in a black suit, grabbed Mae's elbow and walked her over and into one vehicle. T was waiting inside.

"Mae! We're so glad you made it back in one piece!"

"Thank you. It's good to be back on U.S. soil."

"I imagine you're exhausted."

Mae sighed, wearily. "Why did you send me there? It was a complete waste of time."

T stammered for a moment as their SUV pulled away. "We thought that...well, that perhaps your relationship with Tsang would engender their cooperation."

"Why didn't you tell me that before you sent me? They weren't having any of it."

"Um... let's just say we wanted you to be — how should I say this — as authentic as possible. Do you follow?"

"It was terrible, T. Don't ever do that to me again. They sent out these two punks..."

T chuckled.

"I fail to find any humor in it. They were rude and insulting. A couple of low ranking clowns. I couldn't believe it when they said Tsang sent them. He's totally lost my trust."

"Don't be too hard on him. Tsang has his bosses, too."

"Then they dumped me out in the middle of some Shanghai ghetto. I was absolutely terrified, T. I could have been assaulted or something."

"Let's not get carried away, Mae. I apologize for everything that's happened to you. We had no idea they would behave that rudely. The Chinese have been behaving very undiplomatic, recently. All the channels are shutting down since we scaled back the embassy. You should have seen how difficult it was to get out documents out of there."

"Why'd they even bother to meet me?"

"Tsang sounded amenable so we expected a good-faith negotiation. But in the final assessment, I think all his bosses really wanted to do was to insult us. You know, give us the finger. I'm so sorry it all came down on you."

Mae believed T was sincere. "So what happens now?"

T pondered Mae's question as their SUV roared across the sea of concrete and into a shaded parking garage at the farthest edge of the tarmac. Their lane descended underground, away from the bright blue sky and into the shadows of a catacomb. T didn't answer her until the SUV stopped at a checkpoint.

"Things are very shaky right now, Mae. We are truly on the razor's edge."

"It sounded to me like they want to stick it to us.""Probably. The problem for us really isn't China, so much. We know what they've been up to with their recent liquidations. The real issue is Japan. They'll be out of cash in a matter of weeks and we don't know if they'll monetize their debt or start selling off assets to make their interest payments. If they start selling, they'll start with U.S. Treasuries because they know China is getting out. China knows we'll try to buy them up so they'll try to unload theirs at the same time. They'll want to get something for them before it's too late. We'll have to take steps to ensure the whole market doesn't get whored up too fast."

"What's 'too fast'?"

"We're hoping for...well...we've been calling for an orderly crash. We have to manage things, slow things down so the banks can get out. If the banks get caught hanging in too long then it could be a scary correction. We're talking the mother of all bank runs, 1930 times ten. Money markets'll break the buck. Mutual funds will dissolve. Pensions, government payrolls, AR factoring, inventories, everything is at risk if the panic spreads. The Fed will have to take over the entire financial sector and guarantee everything — monetize everything. It'll be a titanic mess."

"When would this start happening? Are we talking about months?"

T shook his head. Mae knew that to mean weeks or days.

"It'll be a selloff of unprecedented magnitude."

The checkpoint guard raised the arm and their SUV passed out of the last of the ambient natural light and fully into the depths of the underground complex.

"The Fed can slow it down with the Plunge Protection Team working through their Wall Street partners. They can buy up whatever the Japanese and Chinese sell with key-stroked, digital cash, but the huge volumes will trigger manual overrides and a 'get out while you can' mentality. With living, breathing, animal spirits at the controls, it all becomes an unpredictable confidence game."

"So are the insiders moving into cash?"

"I'm afraid no. They know that once it goes, it'll take the dollar down with it."

"How far down?"

"We're looking at a fifty to sixty percent devaluation over maybe two weeks or so. If the Fed can't contain it, it'll be a full scale currency collapse."

"What are we going to do?"

"Our job is to make sure it looks more like Argentina and less like the Weimar Republic or Zimbabwe."

Mae shook her head in disbelief. "What about the stock market?"

"When the Treasuries go, corporate paper will follow. Rates will explode. We expect the selloff to trigger circuit breakers and limit downs. The containment plan is fluid, but if it happens three straight days, then we'll shut the whole thing down — call it a 'Market Holiday'. Banks will be closed, accounts will be frozen, capital controls implemented while we sort things out."

"What are all the sheeple going to do, T?"

"Sheeple?" T chuckled. "I guess you didn't get the memo. The new codeword for the John Q Public is 'The Herd'. As you can imagine, they're going be pretty pissed off when their 401ks disappear and their debit cards stop working. The Joint Chiefs expect riots. But we can

31

leverage that by coming to the rescue. Never let a crisis go to waste. The Cabinet's got ideas. First, blame the Chinese. The Herd always falls for a scapegoat. Then, nationalize the retirement accounts and guarantee returns. They call that the Ghialarducci Plan. They'll take all the 401k accounts and reinvest them into Treasuries. That'll soften the blow a little and buy some time for a return to normalcy."

"And...?"

"It's going to be scary, Mae. Did I say that already? How should I describe idea number three? Hmmm. Let's just call it 'law and order maintenance.'"

"Martial Law?"

"The President just initiated 'Operation Pre-emptive Order'. He's recalling and reassigning troops from III Corps. Fourth Infantry actually arrives tomorrow so that confirms that he's taking the hard line. He's not going to let a civil war happen on his watch. Can you imagine a legacy like that?"

"I don't suppose I'll be allowed to get my money out?"

"I'm afraid not, Mae. That would create an audit trail. It's too risky to let government insiders sell right now. We can't risk any questions about integrity. But don't worry, you'll be made whole, inflation-adjusted of course"

The black SUV parked. The driver whispered something into his collar. The door locks clicked open. The chamber was poorly lit, cast in an orange glow. Mae sensed a faint electrical buzzing emanating from all directions. The SUV's cooling exhaust ticked and pinged. An over-sized steel door, painted bright, blood red, stood before them.

Buzz.

Tick. Tick. Tick.

A mechanical noise, like an engagement of industrial gears, rolled and rumbled beneath them. Mae it was unsettled by it.

Buzz.

Tick.

The gears rolled beneath them.

The red door stood before Mae, framed by the windshield of the SUV, partly obstructed by the silhouette of the driver's motionless head.

"So what now?" Mae asked T whose silence was adding to her growing sense of dread.

"The President wants us to stay away from Washington for now," he answered. "So we've set up operations here. Have you been down here? This is a terrific facility. It's like a Hilton. There's a gym, even tennis courts, fine dining. You could move all the essential functions of Washington here. It's quite safe, totally impenetrable."

"It's a bunker."

"There's not a lot for you to do right now but we've made arrangements for you to stay."

"In Denver?"

"Here, in this complex, right through that red door."

Mae felt uneasy. This was the first time she didn't feel comfortable with T. The thought of holing up in a security complex in the bowels of an airport did not appeal to her. She had an urge to dart out of the SUV and sprint up the ramp to the surface, into the air, under the powder blue sky. She would, of course, never indulge such a compulsion.

"Would you mind if I stayed downtown, perhaps the Brown Palace?"

T seemed disappointed. "Not downtown, Mae. It might not be safe. We can make arrangements at a hotel nearby for a few days, I suppose. Then you'll either need to come in here or make your own arrangements. We cannot guarantee your safety if you stay outside the airport complex."

"What do you mean by 'guarantee my safety'?"

"We haven't ruled out TMD."

"TMD?"

"Total Melt Down."

"What do you mean?"

"The President is quite confident we can maintain law and order but there is still a risk."

"How much risk?"

"NSA simulations estimate a one in six chance."

"Of what?"

"Of complete economic and institutional collapse: banking, government, police, fire, hospitals, transportation."

"You can't be serious"

"I only said a one in six chance. Like I said, the President is committed to take any action necessary to maintain law and order. Don't forget, his legacy is at stake."

"So you suggest I stay here?"

"I personally wouldn't play Russian Roulette, so yes, at least until things settle down a bit."

Mae gazed again at the red door. The silhouette of the driver's head leaned forward as he whispered something inaudible into his collar.

Buzz.

Tick.

The grinding gear noise rolled beneath them again.

Mae felt that the shadows had somehow crept in around their SUV. The lights had been gradually dimming. Her queasiness grew.

"I don't want to stay here in this catacomb, T. Can you drive me to one of those nearby hotels for now? I think I might have a safe place to go from there but I have to make some arrangements."

Chapter 6

For seven straight days, Marzan and Rollins remained at their Shariastan firebase. It was an unusual respite which they spent playing first person shooter video games and watching baseball. They learned that the Washington Nationals baseball team had gone bankrupt. Thankfully, Congress came to the rescue, funding the multimillion dollar payroll with federal taxpayer money while a new ownership search committee was organized. Congress justified the nationalization of the Nationals on the grounds that the continued existence of the team "saved jobs". The hundred or so minimum wage concessionaire jobs were indeed "saved" — at a taxpayer cost of over a million dollars each.

Sunday morning, they were ordered to fall in at the mess hall. Another platoon passed Marzan and Rollins as they approached the cafeteria doors. Jimmy noticed bewildered looks on their faces as they shuffled by in silence. None of them were willing to respond when questioned.

When Marzan and Rollins and the others in their platoon had taken their seats, and after the prior platoon's footfalls could no longer be heard in the hallway, Captain Rick appeared. The cafeteria doors were closed and locked behind him.

"Gentlemen, we have a new mission," he announced. But he said it in a peculiar way as if it pained him to say it. This peculiarity dampened any exuberance that might have been percolating in the moods of the twenty eight men in the room who had heard rumors that they might possibly be going home. Rick's announcement dampened everyone's mood except for Jimmy Rollins who let out an ecstatic shout. But he abruptly recoiled under Captain Rick's intense, disapproving glare.

Something was definitely off in the Captain's tone, but little could be gleaned from the eight minute briefing he gave other than instructions on what to pack, what to leave, and when they were leaving which was to be within hours. They weren't told where they were going. Pakistan? Africa? Everyone had a theory. Rollins suggested South America to Marzan, as things had been flaring up there recently. "There's plenty of 'little brown people' to shoot at over there, too," he whispered.

At the conclusion of the briefing, the cafeteria doors were unlocked and flung open and the platoon spilled out into the hallway, silently passing the next curious unit on its way in. They were given two hours to pack their things into pods. They finished with military efficiency and climbed into their Humvees. Jimmy gleaned that they were headed for the airport by the road they took out of the firebase Green Zone. There was no Elvis playing on this trip.

En route, Rollins and Marzan's Humvee got into a little accident with an unfortunate civilian motorcyclist. Another motorist had cut him off and he veered directly into and under their wheels when they tried to swerve out of the way. The entire convoy came to a nerve-racking and dangerous halt along the major Shariastan thoroughfare. The road to the airport was not a safe place to be stalled as there were many upper-storey windows from which opportunistic snipers could take pot shots. It is very difficult to pick out the origin of sniper fire in an urban canyon.

Regardless of all that, someone had to go investigate the situation and give aid to, or at least identify, the victim. Rollins volunteered — he always volunteered — to check things out. Getting out of the scorching Humvee was always a refreshing change of pace. Jimmy Marzan guessed that Rollins was hoping for some blood and gore that might erase a week of dullness. To Jimmy's chagrin, Rollins volunteered him to go along.

"I don't want to be standing around out there for long," Jimmy said as he hopped out onto the street. "They probably think we ran him down on purpose."

"Don't be a pussy," said Rollins.

"Look, they're already closing in."

Rollins approached the victim first. He was most definitely dead as indicated by the mangling of his torso and the black pool radiating out from him on the asphalt. Rollins hovered over the corpse to take a closer look.

"Holy shit, Jimmy! This dude is seriously fucked up," he observed, as he knelt down beside the mangled body and picked through his bloody pockets for ID. "Come check this out."

Jimmy kept his distance, scanning the open windows for RPGs and muzzle flash. The crowd of bystanders drew in around them. "God damn, that was fast," Jimmy thought as they gathered. He glanced quickly at the corpse. It didn't even seem to be human. It resembled road kill.

Jimmy was initially pleased by his immediate sensation of

disconnectedness at the sight of the body. To see a twisted and mangled man, shredded by the torqueing forces of a Humvee's 300-pound wheels, blood and brains splattered up into the wheel wells, and not feel any recoil at the gruesomeness, was a testament to his military hardening. He had become numb to gore. But he discovered that he was not yet fully numb to remorse. Jimmy's eyes moved to scanning the open windows in the surrounding buildings in an effort to block it out, but the dead man's humanity had already infected his mind. This man probably had a family. He had a mother. Maybe he had a wife, a brother, even children. Perhaps these children were playing in front of their house, waiting for their daddy, oblivious to the horrible news that would soon rip their lives apart.

Jimmy drove the thoughts out of his mind. He had been conditioned by the Army and he knew how to deaden destructive thoughts like these. The indigenous people were just things, not beings, things that often were, or gave aid and comfort to, the enemy.

Whenever a flicker of pity sparked in Jimmy's mind, he remembered his dead brothers-in-arms. He remembered Private Fossen from Savannah, whose head exploded out the back when he was picked off by a sniper. And there was Roberts from Jacksonville, who was cooked alive in his Humvee after the concussion of an IED explosion warped the truck's iron doors shut, sealing him inside an oven oven. Jimmy could still hear his faint screams, muffled by the armor and the roar of the fire. Then there was Michaels from Austin who bled out so fast that the transfusion of milky fake blood oozed out of his fist-sized chest wound before the medics gave up on administering CPR. Michaels had mystical azure eyes. In his death, they appealed to God. Those pale blue gemstones, set within his pearly, exsanguinated face; Michaels had the gaze of an angel. He stared stared forever in Jimmy's memory.

And that was how soldiers were conditioned. Before long, Jimmy Marzan felt no more pity for the mangled 'little brown man.'

"Check this out. Mmm!" mocked Rollins as he removed his knife from his belt and pretended to scoop out a portion of brain matter from the deceased's exploded skull as if his head were a breakfast melon.

Marzan wasn't amused.

The platoon soon handed the scene off to the local police and went on their way. Within three hours, they were buckled into the leather seats of a commercial jetliner. They sipped lemon-lime soda in their sweaty fatigues and read about the latest popular vacation destinations in the magazines tucked in the seat pockets in front of them. Their rifles were stowed in the overhead bins, and they were reminded by flight attendants — with fluttering fake eyelashes and pancake makeup and long, polished fingernails — to "take care when opening the overhead compartments as contents may have shifted during flight."

Liberty Air, also recently nationalized when teetering at the precipice of insolvency, had managed something of a resurgence under her new American-taxpayer ownership. An infinite bankroll can do that for a company. Liberty, unlike the other airlines that had recently disappeared, had facilities in all the right congressional districts, districts with all the right congressmen whose campaigns were funded by all the right donors — all the right union donors. Thus Liberty was saved and the other airlines, most in better financial condition, were left to die.

So what about Liberty's creditors? You know, the ones that poured in billions trying to keep their investment aloft? "To hell with those greedy bastards," was the congressional attitude. Those "greedy bastards," the owners, who were in reality just middle-class Americans with retirement accounts, got tossed out the hatch without a parachute. Liberty Air sailed on with her new union co-owners, her monetary debts forgiven by Congress. Soon after the restructuring, Liberty magically secured the very lucrative deal of ferrying U.S. soldiers around the globe-spanning empire.

So, there Jimmy sat on that Airbus, next to Michael Rollins who was asleep most of the time, with drool trickling down his chin. They made a short stop in Frankfurt, then they were airborne again. They flew over England. *It apparently isn't going to be South America after all. Rollins will be so disappointed,* thought Jimmy. *But where are we headed, then?*

No one knew anything for a fact. Or if they knew, they weren't talking. Not even that beady-eyed PFC Black was talking. *And that smug, little weasel knew everything,* thought Jimmy.

They seemed to be flying due west but it was hard to tell as they were above a blanket of clouds. *Maybe Mexico?* That made sense. *It was just a matter of time before their chaos sucked us in.*

Jimmy fell asleep reading a story about how the country's economy could be saved by "green jobs." Congress planned to pass a law requiring every window in the country be replaced with a newly-developed, energy-efficient, hi-tech glass. What a boon to the window glaziers!

When Jimmy awoke, he first glanced over at Rollins who was still asleep and drooling. Then he took a look out the portal window where he saw that the clouds had cleared away. Their plane was descending. Far off on the horizon stood the Statue of Liberty.

Chapter 7

"Are you MS13?" asked Undersheriff Garrity, referring to the violent street gang that had infiltrated Jefferson County. He knew it was so, based on the 'MS13' tattoo inked into the suspect's forehead. Joe Joe, as he was nicknamed, was a potential bonanza of information regarding all the recent kidnappings and unsolved murders taking place in the County.

The bleeding hearts had blamed the rash of brazen lawlessness on the poor economy. Garrity thought differently. "It's those immigrants causing all the trouble," he often lamented. Now he had one he could interrogate. Garrity was on a mission. He wanted leads. Leads led to arrests. Arrests led to newspaper clippings and public adulation. Public adulation filled the void of loneliness consuming his soul.

Joe Joe finally answered. "Fock you, Fatman."

Garrity felt his polyester uniform stretching taut between the buttons. He didn't like being reminded of his weight, that made him self-conscious. His tense energy manifested itself in his hands which fidgeted and made their way to the top of his head, feeling for the spot where his hair was thinning out. After realizing it, he yanked his arm down and rested it on the table. He resented himself for his inability to control his unconscious displays of weakness. And he didn't appreciate being insulted by a suspect during an interrogation. Contempt-of-cop was a direct challenge to his status as a high-ranking, county law enforcer. He didn't have a lot of tolerance for disrespect.

"Who are you with, Joe Joe?" Garrity asked him, his pudgy face beginning to smolder.

"I say fock you," Joe Joe replied defiantly. He puffed up the torso of his five-foot-three frame and smiled mockingly, revealing a mouthful of silvery dental work.

Garrity sighed. His chubby cheeks blushed with his building rage.

"What gang are you with?"

"I no hablo Ingleis."

Garrity discovered his hand had found its way back to his bald patch again. *God dammit,* he thought as he yanked it down again.

"You hablo ingleis just fine, Joe Joe. I know who you are. Who do you run with, these days? Romero?"

Joe Joe just grinned his silvery grin.

"Why weren't you packing?"

"Cuz shooting gringos'll get you the electric chair."

"You're right on that, Joe Joe," Garrity answered as he leaned back, interlocking his chunky fingers behind his head so they wouldn't meander. The armpits of his polyester uniform were marked with patches of sweat. "So," he continued, "you break into this guy's house solo, no gun, you knew he was home – what the hell? Other than tattooing your gang onto your face, you shouldn't be that stupido. You been sniffing that spray paint?"

Joe Joe leaned back and tried to stretch his hands up behind his head to mimic Garrity, but his chains snapped tight.

"I no talk to you. I wan my lawyer."

"You'll get your lawyer when you tell me who you're working with these days. Give me some names."

Joe Joe's eyes scowled for a brief second but his face quickly brightened again. "You get my lawyer. I have my right."

"I'll get you something all right," Garrity answered, his cheeks reddening, veins thickening in his temples. As far as Garrity was concerned, rights were just something written on a piece of paper whenever it came to illegal aliens.

"You get my lawyer right now. I no talk to you."

"C'mon, Joe Joe. Don't make this more difficult for yourself."

"You get my lawyer. You get my lawyer, now. I no afraid a you, Fatman. You get my lawyer."

"No. I'm sorry, but not yet Joe Joe," Garrity explained, suppressing his rage. "You're gonna answer some of my questions first."

"You no fock with me, cop. You fock with me, we fock with you back. I have my right."

"Who's 'we', Joe Joe?"

"You fock with me, we fock with you. Comprende?"

"You better watch it, Joe Joe. I'm the sheriff 'round these parts. Sheriffs don't like being threatened, especially by gangbanger illegals. Do *you* comprende?"

Joe Joe rolled his dark brown eyes while Garrity glanced up at the camera tucked into the corner of the interrogation room. He conspicuously did the kill-it slash with an index finger across his throat. The red light indicating the camera was recording turned off. "I'm giving you one last chance, Joe Joe. Who's your boss? What were you looking for in that house? I want information. And I'm warning you, if you don't cooperate, we're going to use another form of interrogation — a more aggressive form. You comprende that?

"You no fock with me," Joe Joe replied. "We know everything bout you, Robert Garrity."

Garrity had enough. He briskly pushed his bloated body up from his chair, took a moment to straighten and calm himself, then slowly walked around the table to Joe Joe's right side.

"You makin a big mistake," Joe Joe warned. "We know where you live — 7700 McKinley Dr."

Garrity snatched Joe's right hand and braced Joe Joe's elbow onto his hip bending Joe Joe's hand down at the wrist at a 90 degree angle, a hold designed to create the sensation of impending wrist dislocation. Joe Joe squirmed.

"You listen to me," Garrity growled. "You don't threaten the sheriff. You threaten me, I'll bust your damn huevos. Understand?"

Joe Joe grunted in pain.

Garrity held his wrist at the precarious angle with his left arm and with his right, he removed his baton from his belt.
Joe Joe groaned.

"Now," continued Garrity as he bent Joe Joe's wrist ever closer to the snapping point, "we're gonna have a conversation which'll involve me asking questions and you answering them. Understand? Now, you're gonna tell me what gang you're with. You're gonna tell me who your boss is. You're gonna give me names and addresses and anything else you know about the kidnappings going on around here lately."

Joe Joe grimaced.

Garrity swung the baton down and jabbed Joe Joe squarely in the groin with the blunt end, not so hard as to cause injury, but with enough force to cause Joe Joe to squeal.

"Who's your boss, Joe Joe?"

Joe Joe held back. Garrity swung the baton down again and Joe Joe let out a croaking noise like the sound someone makes while vomiting.

Garrity prided himself in being an efficient torture-master. He cherished his reputation with the deputies for his willingness to go that extra mile, and although most of them personally disliked and avoided the uninhibited undersheriff, many sought out his talents in especially tough cases. The recent county crime spree had opened the department's minds to techniques of enhanced interrogation. Garrity pretty much considered all cases as especially tough. He employed his enhanced interrogation techniques almost weekly.

He held Joe Joe's handcuffed wrist at the brink of dislocation with one arm, and with the elegance of a symphonic conductor, he hammered Joe Joe in the groin twice more with his baton. Joe Joe wretched and convulsed. He pulled his other cuffed left hand over to shield himself but the chain snapped taut.

"What was that, Joe Joe? Are you resisting?" Garrity asked mockingly. He released Joe Joe's wrist, reached over and grabbed his other hand, pulled it forward and slammed it on the table. With fingers splayed apart, he rapped them with the baton twice so hard that it sounded like he was pounding nails into plywood.

Garrity knew well the limits of prisoner physiology. He was a man fascinated by how the Romans could calculate, within minutes, the time of death of a convict by the gore unleashed in a pre-crucifixion flogging. He admired the science of Roman sadism.

Meanwhile, Joe Joe screamed and ground his silver teeth together in agony.

"You're illegal, Joe Joe. That means you don't exist. You have no rights in this county. That means I can do whatever I want to you. I can even make you disappear if I choose. There's lots of places back in the woods to bury someone where no one would ever find him."

"I no understand," Joe Joe replied.

"You think you're a tough, eh? I know you understand just fine. Here, let me see if this makes you remember."

Garrity took out his revolver and set it on the table. He was the only officer in the County that still used a revolver, but Garrity believed that his .357 hand-cannon added to his mystique. At one point, he had nicknamed himself "Dirty Garrity".

He reached into his pocket and pulled out a cartridge and showed it to Joe Joe. Then he picked up the pistol, placed the bullet into a chamber and spun the cylinder, holding the barrel down. Unbeknownst to Joe Joe, he didn't actually put the bullet in the gun, he was only a borderline psychotic. Instead, he deftly dropped it into his sleeve like a magician. But the effect of his Russian Roulette technique on suspects was usually profound. Garrity had employed it many times to coax suspects into confession.

Garrity put the gun into Joe Joe's mouth, jamming it way in, deep enough to trigger his gag reflex. Although in great pain, Joe Joe had not shown any fear until this moment. He now had the a look of terror that garrity had seen in the eyes of a gazelle just at the point where a lion has just latched onto its neck and dug its teeth in. Garrity thoroughly enjoyed watching predation on the Discovery Channel.

Joe Joe mumbled Latin prayers as he choked on the barrel of the revolver jammed into his mouth. "Now Joe Joe, are you gonna cooperate?"

Joe Joe just prayed.

"I'm gonna count to three..."

Joe Joe said nothing.

"One..."

Joe Joe closed his eyes.

"Two..."

Joe Joe held his breath.

"Three..."

Garrity growled as he squeezed the trigger.

Click.

Disappointed, Garrity removed the .357 from Joe Joe's mouth.

Joe Joe held his eyes closed and resumed praying. His left hand was beginning to swell. He was hyperventilating between verses.

"Joe Joe," Garrity whispered in his ear, "I've got something to show you. Open your eyes. Yeah, that's it." Garrity went back to his side of the table and took his seat. "Look here. Look what I've brought for you." Garrity reached under the table and produced a gray, hard shell briefcase and set it on the table before him. "Do you know what I've got in here, Joe Joe? Huh? Can you guess? Why don't you guess for me, Joe Joe. Take a wild guess."

Joe Joe trembled, sweating, eyes flitting about, his shaved head and tattoos and patchy beard no longer gave him any aura of toughness. He looked less like an MS13 thug and more like some drugged up schizophrenic in a psych ward.

"Joe Joe, I want to tell you about this little present I have for you in this briefcase. You see, when I worked for vice back in DC, we used to bust these S&M outfits all the time. Well, I came across this one day, and I decided that I just had to hang on to it. You never know when something might come in handy. Know what I mean? Then it dawned on me. Yeah, it dawned on me that what I have in this briefcase would make a very persuasive tool for interrogation."

Joe Joe stared at the case.

"Joe Joe, have you ever heard of Steely Dan?"

Joe Joe shook his head.

"No, you probably haven't, have you. All you Mexicans listen to that ranchera music, don't ya?" Joe Joe was actually from El

Salvador. Garrity went on for a few moments impersonating a trumpet player humming La Cucaracha. He continued, "Steely Dan is a rock and roll band, Joe Joe. Not one of my personal favorites as they are a little jazzy for my taste. They had a hit song back in the seventies called "Black Friday." Ever hear it? No? Well Joe Joe, I'm here to let you know that today is your personal Black Friday."

Garrity took out his baton again and rapped it on the table three times. The door opened and in burst two deputies clad in head to toe black polyester. They had an SS aura about them. "Uncuff him," Garrity ordered.

The two deputies freed Joe Joe from the chair but held his arms tightly.

"Let me tell you something, Joe Joe. Steely Dan is not just a rock and roll band," Garrity explained as he clicked the briefcase open. "The name Steely Dan has an origin. Do you know what it is? No, of course you don't." He opened the lid of the case. Sweat rolled down Joe Joe's forehead and into his eyes. Garrity spun the case around on the table. Joe Joe looked inside but what was there was covered with black felt. "Can we get this on video?" Garrity asked. "I think maybe Joe Joe's fellow gangbangers would like to see this. No, not the room camera. Who's got the best camera phone?"

One of the deputies took his phone out of his pocket and began to record the scene.

"Go ahead, Joe Joe," Garrity continued. "Take a look under the felt. Check it out."

Joe Joe remained frozen in terror.

Everyone jumped as Garrity picked up his baton and rapped it on the table again.

"Look inside!" He shouted.

Joe Joe extended his good hand. Reaching into the case, he pulled off the felt cloth. He instantly recoiled back in his chair. "No! No! No!" he shouted as he tried to break loose of the officers holding him.

"Yes! Yes! Yes!" Garrity replied with a sinister grin. "Now you know all about the Steely Dan. And now it's time, Joe Joe. It's time to assume the position."

The officers bent Joe Joe over the table. Garrity came around to his side again and leaned down into Joe Joe's face which was smashed flat against the metal surface.

"Isn't this how they do it back home?" Garrity asked.

Joe Joe's eyes filled with tears.

"Well? Isn't it?"

"I tell you! I tell you! I tell you everything," Joe Joe sobbed.

"Too late, Joe Joe. I wonder what your buddies will think of this video."

"No! No! I tell you! I tell you! Please. He prayed again in Spanish. "I tell you. I tell you what I stealing."

"He didn't ask you about that," barked one of the officers.

But Joe Joe's comment fired a synapse in Garrity's mind, stinging him as if he were chewing on tinfoil. As a lifetime civil servant, Garrity had evolved into a finely-tuned opportunist. He wanted to learn more about Joe Joe's attempted theft. It had to be something good. "What are you talking about, Joe Joe?"

"I tell you what I steal. I tell you. Good news for you. I tell if you stop. Okay?"

Garrity let Joe Joe grovel and pray for a few moments.

"Okay. Tell me. Go!" Garrity finally ordered.

"Okay. I go. Here, here it is. I hear from some dealer I know that this man got these coin — a whole lot a them."

"Coins? Since when are you Mexicans into coin collections? The only things I've ever seen you guys collect are those velvet bullfighter paintings."

"I know. It sound funny. I hear it from dealer. We're no talking cheap coin. We're talking bout gold coin...Krugerrand. The man I rob, he buy from my dealer friend and he tell me so I go to that man's house to get them. Fifty thousand dollars, he said."

"Bullshit. You were goin there to get his daughter."

"No! No! I no kidnap. I no kidnap no kid. I no pedofilo. I kill them pedofilo." Joe Joe spat. "I no lie. He have fifty thousand. Price go up every day. Monday up. Tuesday up. Wednesday up. Price go up every day."

"He's full of it," interjected one of the deputies.

"Shut up!" Garrity snapped as he sat down and leaned back in his chair in contemplation. He pondered how he might use this new knowledge. *It's was probably bullshit,* he thought. *But then again, fifty thousand in gold?*

"Why'd you go there when he was home? Why not wait till the house was empty?"

"'Cause I leaving for El Salvador that morning. I get out of the gang. I no wanna kill no one. I just need money."

"Cuff him again," Garrity ordered.

"So that's it?" whined the other Nazi with flaring nostrils.

"If you really want some Steely Dan, perhaps we could practice on you?" Garrity replied.

The two officers cuffed Joe Joe behind his back.

"You gonna tell me who your dealer friend is?"

"He a pawn dealer. It all check out."

"Get him out of here, then. And get him some ice for his hand."

"Should we have it x-rayed?"

"It ain't broke. I know what I'm doing."

The two deputies hustled Joe Joe out of the interview room and into a cell.

Chapter 8

Vaughn suffered from chronic insomnia since the home invasion weeks before. The slightest noises disturbed his slumber and he found himself patrolling the house with his shotgun at least once every night. Jessica, on the other hand, was able to fall asleep without much difficulty, which added to Vaughn's frustration. After his nighttime patrols, he would spend the remainder of his night channel surfing. Lack of sleep was beginning to affect his personality as he was growing increasingly fixated on the radio and television reports of daily five to ten percent moves in the global markets.

The exchanges would almost always start the day with steep crashes at the opening bell, sinking like a stone. The talking heads in the media would hysterically announce, "Flash Crash! Flash Crash! Here we go again! Someone has to do something about those program traders!" After dropping five percent, the market would magically reverse course, rocketing up from the depths like a buoy spit out by some giant fish. Once fully rebounded, the talking heads would return to sobriety, as if nothing had happened.

Vaughn was completing his evening patrol when he decided to pour himself a quadruple Wild Turkey nightcap before flipping on the television. He turned on one of the business channels. The pictures of panicked Asian faces flailing about piqued his curiosity. Something very newsworthy was happening. Vaughn turned up the volume.

"...the selloff started about midway through the session with rumors swirling about the cash-strapped Bank of Japan liquidating half of their U.S. Treasury holdings. Prices on the U.S. ten-year plunged, taking yields up one hundred basis points over the span of about eight minutes. Record volume led one trader to speculate that the Central Banks of the U.K., Saudi Arabia, and China were stepping in to halt a possible U.S. bond collapse. Yields seemed to level off for about half an hour, but then the frantic selloff resumed driving ten-year Treasury yields up another whopping 190 basis points." repoted an Australian analyst.

"So what impact has this had on the currency markets?" asked the anchor. "Is everyone moving into dollars?"

"Well, the conventional wisdom is that such a dramatic move down in Treasuries would drive many investors into U.S. dollars as a safe haven, but that has not been the case today. There is a dollar sell-off happening concurrently with the greenback down almost ten percent against the yen and euro, and off a whopping fifteen percent against the Chinese yuan. These are all unprecedented moves."

"What are the Chinese doing?"

"Normally, the People's Bank of China keeps the yuan pegged to the dollar with controlled adjustments, but they're not intervening. The yuan is taking off. "

"Where are the investors going, then? What's the safe haven?"

"Yeah," nodding and holding earpiece, "well, it's been a huge day for metals, agricultural commodities, and oil. Oil is up almost fifty dollars during the session."

"Wow. So, what happens now?"

"Hmm," holding earpiece again. "well, with commodity futures still climbing and Treasuries still tanking, it looks like the bloodbath will continue when the DAX opens."

"Thank you...Uh huh...One moment...(holding ear)...Uh, we've just received word that the Federal Reserve will be holding an emergency session in..."

Vaughn was struck with uneasiness by the spaced-out look in the reporter's eyes. He sensed this was the genesis of something most unpleasant. It just had that kind of feeling about it, like when he first saw that black smoke billowing out of the World Trade Center. He didn't know what to do about it but his gut told him to do *something*.

"Jess! Jess! Wake up!"

Jessica popped up in bed, eyes wide in terror. "What's going on?"

"We have to go to the grocery store."

"What?"

"We have to go to the grocery store. C'mon, get up."

"Vaughn, no. What's wrong with you? It's the middle of the night."

"We have to go to the grocery store, Jess. I'm not leaving you here alone. It's not an option. C'mon, get up. I'll get Brooke ready."

With a little further prodding, Jessica dragged herself from bed and got dressed. But she let her displeasure be known with a series of sighs and scowls. In the background, the television droned on about the crash contagion that was spreading to the Indian markets.

"Why are we doing this, Vaughn?"

"It's beginning," he explained. "Listen to the TV. I think we should stock up on some things before morning. We should fill up on

50

gas and get some groceries and stuff. There might be a panic. Your prescription's running low, too."

"What's happening?"

"The day of reckoning has come."

Jessica rolled her eyes. But she went along with the drill because ever since the break-in, Vaughn had become obsessive about preparedness. Resistance was futile. He would not let her go back to sleep if she refused to go along. Vaughn loaded his family into his pickup in the darkness and they set off. Brooke fell immediately back to sleep.

Vaughn flipped from station to station on the radio as they drove, searching for market updates. Classic rock. Hip hop. Traffic report at 1 am. "Why do they have traffic reports at 1 am?" Vaughn switched to the AM band: infomercial for vitamins...in search of Chupacabra...business news. "Finally, a business station!"

"...the foreign market volume is extremely heavy — record levels. The yen plunged first then bounced, then the dollar just absolutely tanked. I've never seen the dollar move like that. The Chinese yuan is up sharply, as much as thirty percent..."

"Will you please tell me what's going on?" Jessica asked.

"This is the big one!" Vaughn offered. "Is Anderson's open twenty-four hours?"

"They closed down a month ago. You have to go to King's."

Either way, it was a seven-mile drive on winding country roads in the dead of night. They made it in twelve minutes. Vaughn expected to find a calamity of cars in the lot but it was nearly empty. Jess rolled her eyes at the lack of panic.

Vaughn dropped Jess off at the front entrance and pulled into the gas station. Only one other car was there. Thankfully, the gas prices were the same as the day before. "Whew." It was probably a little crazy to think the manager would have come out and raised them in the middle of the night, Vaughn thought as he slid his credit card through the pump's swiper and waited for it to process.

He waited...

...and he waited.

He swiped again...

...and he waited.

Brooke started to get restless. Vaughn watched her rousing in her car seat through the side window. He checked the card indicator again.

"Card Failed To Read"

Vaughn swiped his card again. He didn't have any cash and there wasn't any attendant to pay at that hour, anyway. The reader processed again. *Could it be that the banks had been closed or electronic transactions had been frozen to stop bank runs or something?* he thought.

"C'mon, God damn it," he muttered, realizing that he might not have enough gas to get home.

"Card Processing..."

Brooke was awake and looking at him from her car seat. Her lower lip began to hang in a pout like it always did when she was about to start crying. Next would be the chin quiver, then a full-throttle wail. He made a funny face at her which made her smile. Crisis temporarily averted.

"Come on!" he barked at the pump.

"Card Processing..."

What will I do if I don't have enough gas to get home? It was a seven-mile walk in the darkness through mountain lion country with a two-year-old in tow. He checked out the other car.

"Hey!" Vaughn shouted towards the other patron. "Is your pump working?"

"No! It doesn't seem to want to read my card."

"God damn it," Vaughn whispered to himself. "Do you think they've closed the banks?" he asked.

"Huh?" answered the other patron. He was obviously not up to date on the Asian markets crash.

"Never mind," Vaughn replied.

"Pump Authorizing..."

"Thank God!" Vaughn shouted as the pump clicked on and the nectar of capitalism began to flow into his tank. After topping off, Vaughn pulled in to the front of the grocery store. He took Brooke in, set her gently into a shopping cart and cushioned her with her blanket and her monkey. A handful of people were grazing around inside, a few more than one would expect for that time of night, but certainly not a panicked mob of hoarders. Vaughn was a little bit disappointed by that as he felt that the presence of a chaotic throng might somehow validate his insistence on dragging his family out in the middle of the night.

What should we buy? he asked himself as he scanned the rows. He started to the right in produce, but produce doesn't keep so he didn't gather anything there except for some grapes which Brooke liked. He worked his way down the dairy end but that too seemed to be a poor choice for a doomsday stockpile. With his cart still empty, and Brooke slumped to one side, asleep, he skipped the greeting card aisle and turned down the next row — paper products. It was there that he ran into his next-door neighbor, a man he had never spoken too and whose name he had forgotten, but whom he recognized by his straw cowboy hat and long wiry beard. Vaughn stopped and took note of the contents of his neighbor's cart which was jammed to overflowing. He must have been working back Vaughn's way from the other direction. It contained, among other things: several boxes of oatmeal, a couple bags of rice, dried pasta, instant potatoes, dozens upon dozens of cans of vegetables and fruits, sugar, flour, vegetable oil, peanut butter, cans of tuna, spam and chicken, box after box of macaroni and cheese, a large brown bottle of hydrogen peroxide, bandages and iodine

His neighbor apparently had things figured out.

"Howdy," Vaughn said as his neighbor scanned the top shelf. "It looks like you're stocking up for something."

Their eyes met. Vaughn glanced admiringly at his neighbor's hoard. His neighbor nodded and smiled back, tipping his straw hat.

"I think I'm your neighbor. I'm Vaughn Clayton."

"Good evening to you," he answered with a nod. I'm Ian Croukamp."

"What brings you out at this time of night?" Vaughn asked.

"The radio," he answered bluntly, with an odd quality to his enunciation.

"Hear about the stuff going on in Asia?"

"Indeed."

"Oh I'm happy to hear I'm not the only one. I'm surprised there aren't more people in here stocking up."

Croukamp chuckled, "They won't panic just yet."
Vaughn detected a British accent, kind of British, but not quite. "Why's that?" Vaughn asked.

"Huh?"

"Why no panic?"

"Because CNN hasn't told them to panic, yet," he explained.

Vaughn laughed uncomfortably. "So what brings you out here at night if there isn't any panic?" Vaughn persisted.

"A day early is better than a minute late. I'm stocking up before they change the prices."

"So you *do* think something's happening?"

"I hope not, but I expect so. I'd like to get some of that toilet paper in case it goes up to $25 a roll. Can you reach that bundle up there for me?"

Vaughn reached up and pushed an eighteen pack off the shelf. Croukamp caught it and stacked it on top of his cart.

"So what do you think'll happen?" Vaughn asked.

"It's just like back home."

"Where's that?"

"Rhodesia."

"Oh, you mean Zimbabwe?"

"I mean Rhodesia."

"No kidding? Were you there when the inflation hit? That must have been a quite an experience."

"Mugabe. There aren't ample words to describe that man. Murdering, Marxist butcher is insufficient."

Vaughn recognized that he was getting way out of line with his questions. He tried to rein things in a little. "So, do you have any suggestions for me? What should I stock up on?"

"Oh, I don't do that."

"Please. I have no clue what to get."

Croukamp scratched his head but finally answered. "Buy some Krugerrands. Lots of them. Ten, twenty, fifty ounces ought to get you started. That will help protect you a little. Good evening and good luck to you." Croukamp pushed off down the aisle and disappeared around the end.

Vaughn ran into Jess about halfway through the store. She was filling her own cart and had built a surprisingly good hoard considering her doomsday skepticism. Her cart was nearly full with non-perishables with the exception of a few indulgences like potato chips. Her prescription was filled as well. They decided that they had accumulated enough of a stash for one night and proceeded to the checkout lane.

In the line ahead, a chubby fellow with long hair pulled back into a pony tail was unloading his cart onto the conveyor belt. He built an assembly line of liters of soda pop and frozen waffles. Then hot dogs, French bread, tomatoes, eggs, yogurt, three frozen pizzas, shrimp cocktail, hair conditioner...

"Excuse me," interrupted another voice from behind them. Turning, Vaughn saw a slight fellow hiding behind dark sunglasses and a ball cap. "Mind if I cut in front of you?" he asked, presumptively pushing his cart through before Vaughn had even responded. "I only have a couple things and I'm in quite a hurry."

"Sure," Vaughn answered reflexively. His cart contained three bottles of designer water, three individually wrapped, miniature, gourmet cheeses, and a bottle of baby lotion.

"Rudy, can you assist checkout?" barked the clerk impatiently into the intercom.

Jessica pulled Vaughn back towards her and whispered in his ear. "Do you know who that is?"

"Who? That guy there?"

"Shhhh. He'll hear you. Don't stare. Yeah, him."

"I have no idea, Jess. Is he from your spinning class or something?"

"No, stupid. That's Johnny McDouglas."

"Johnny McDouglas? The actor?"

"Yep."

"You're on drugs."

"Look at him!" Jessica whispered emphatically.

Vaughn looked him over again. He was maybe five foot six. He was very thin, but square-shouldered. He was dressed casually but not cheaply. His sweats were label. His black sweater was silk and he was wearing Bruno Magli shoes—OJ loafers. He sensed that McDouglas was aware of it but was trying to act oblivious, the way celebrities act when they don't want to be pestered by obnoxious, laypeople.

Jessica yanked on Vaughn's arm, again, but he kept staring, searching for additional signs of Hollywood royalty. The alleged Mr. McDouglas had manicured, almost feminine hands. He wore a silver chain bracelet which was a rare accessory for a man to wear in a mountain town. His sunglasses, worn in the middle of the night were another indication. Then the giveaway, a white-gold, Movado watch with its black face and the solitary dot marking twelve o'clock. *Who in the heck would wear a five-thousand-dollar Movado watch to the grocery store at 3 a.m.?*

Whoever he was, he had money.

"I think you may be right," Vaughn whispered back to Jessica.

"It's him."

"How could you tell? The watch?"

"It's the shoes."

"Aha."

"Look around...I bet he's on one of these magazines in here."

"Wow. So he really does live here. I thought that was a myth."

55

Chapter 9

The president appeared on morning television on every channel, even ESPN and HBO. Their executives strongly protested the hastily drafted White House programming order (and usurpation of the First Amendment). "Show it or else..." was the reply from the White House. "The First Amendment does not apply during a national emergency." The resistant networks meekly complied. It's best not to upset the man holding the telecom kill switch.

At first glance, the president's inescapable face appeared to beam strength and resoluteness. His eyes were reassuring, squinting with a confident glint. His navy blue suit and red tie shouted, "I'm in charge! Everything is okay!" He spoke in a smooth, gentle current, smiling often.

But something was askew. His cosmetics were a little off. It seemed too thick or badly retouched or the tone was off—like a dead man's makeup. His shave was not close, and his shoulders slumped a little bit.

He sat behind that familiar White House desk, framed by an American flag and a bureau of family photos and the Oval Office window draped in gold curtains. The window opened out into what appeared to be a quaint, wooded, suburban backyard. Somehow, the sky framed in that window was blue and clear that morning while the rest of Washington D.C. was being bombarded by a deluge of rain.

The Oval Office set—which might have actually been a blue screen on Air Force One for all anyone knew—was designed to conjure images of a fatherly chat in the household study. The president played the role of Ward Cleaver in the minds of the middle class who were obediently awaiting instructions. But the choreographed invocation did not conjure personal memories of real fathers for the audience so much as it conjured a nostalgic vision, implanted into the American mind by the family-themed television shows they absorbed over the course of their lives. The Oval Office chats parroted stylized TV life which itself parroted stylized life of the 1950s. Few had studies in their homes anymore. And most Americans never had a real chat with their real dad while he was dressed in a suit and sitting behind a desk. Many Americans had no memory of meaningful chats with their dads at all, other than superficial conversations every other weekend. And if they were so lucky as to have a real chat with their real dad, the view out the study window would probably be of the siding of the next door neighbor's plywood mcmansion.

Yet so many presidents had given addresses from that fabricated set, apparently because it worked so well. For an audience conditioned by a lifetime of mass media, the conjured image instilled calmness, trust and submissiveness. It made the infantilized and helpless population of dependent serfs feel at ease. "The president is father, and father knows best. Everything will be okay. Just keep doing what you're told."

Vaughn poured himself a cup of coffee as he contemplated calling in sick from work. He was exhausted from running around all night, but he decided he needed to go in. *This is not the time to inconvenience my employer,* he thought. There was twenty percent unemployment out there, by some unofficial accounts.

The president started to speak as Vaughn took his first sip of designer coffee. Good thing he stocked up on the stuff before the Seattle firm went bankrupt.

"My fellow Americans, over the past night, while most of you were sleeping, rogue elements, operating in foreign markets and exchanges—elements unfriendly to America—launched a coordinated surprise attack upon the people of United States. This attack was not one waged by ships and planes or on any battlefield, but it was an attack nonetheless. This was an act of terror, not waged with bombs, but waged by keyboards and the internet and on public trading exchanges. These foreign agents and rogue elements have sought to injure America," he paused for a moment, then smirked, "but they will soon discover that they cannot subdue our great nation by cowardly acts of terrorism. America is a resilient nation. It has survived a Civil War and the Great Depression. It and has mobilized the arsenal of democracy to win two world wars. It's a nation that always rallies, always comes together. America will unite to confront this challenge, as it always has in times of tribulation and struggle. We have the most powerful economy in the world. America is the world's engine of prosperity and growth. Our industriousness and our diversity are the envy of all the nations. And no matter what the forces of evil may attempt in order to harm us, we shall endure. We will vanquish our foes and recover. America has faced adversity and always come back stronger. Tested," he paused for emphasis, "but with greater resolve. Our democracy has always been reborn wiser and stronger by her trials…

Blah, blah, blah, Terrorism...
Blah, blah, blah, Freedom...
Blah, blah, blah, Sacrifice...
Blah, blah, blah, Diversity...
Blah, blah, blah, Progress...
Blah, blah, blah, Responsibility...
Hope...Security...Faith...Future Generations....

Thank you. God bless you and God bless the United States of America."

Presidential speeches never change.

While the president spoke, corporate purchasing agents, who had no time for imperial propaganda, were on the phone with their overseas suppliers. After hanging up, they frantically updated their spreadsheet models with new raw materials costs.

"Holy shit!"

Millions of "Effective Immediately" emails flew out to distribution centers and warehouses and convenience stores and retail outlets. Out in the real world, while the big media talking heads blathered on about the emperor's new clothes, shopkeepers were doubling and tripling the numbers on their price tags, databases and marquees. Prices were rising in real time.

On-the-street reporters, only marginally less vapid then the in-studio anchors, hit the streets seeking to expose the "evil capitalist price gougers" who were using the economic emergency as an opportunity to line their pockets. The reporters shoved microphones and cameras into disgruntled customer faces and captured their lamentations. Grocery store traffic was elevated, but the clerks noticed that the big movers were potato chips and soft drinks and beer. Eat drink and be merry for tomorrow we die.

Local police departments were notified overnight by agents of the Department of Homeland Security and FEMA to increase their presence and visibility. Vaughn noticed two patrol cars cruising through his neighborhood as he got ready for work.

Vaughn's 72-inch, high-definition flat screen made in China droned on. "We have gone past the point of no return," said the chief European economist at the Royal Bank of Scotland. "There is a complete loss of confidence. The bond markets are disintegrating and it is getting worse moment by moment."

"What should the government do?" asked the anchor who couldn't understand why the government had allowed it all to happen.

"The banks need more liquidity. The Central Banks — the Fed, B of E, Bank of Japan — need to create more money and lend it to the commercial banks so they can continue to operate. They have to have the cash to buy up the glut of sovereign debt out there before the system collapses. But first, we need to close the markets and let the Central Banks get together and sort everything out."

"So, more bailouts? What do you say to those who argue that that isn't capitalism — that markets should be allowed to liquidate?"

"We're dealing with the real world here, not some textbook ideology. Call it whatever you like, intervention, QE, whatever, we have to destroy capitalism in order to save capitalism!"

It was quite a morning. The contagion cruise that embarked from Asia — while America snored the night away tucked in their Therapedic, space-foam mattresses purchased on their Visa cards — continued its world tour through China and Australia, past India and the oil fiefs and Europe, across the Atlantic. Markets in India, Russia, Germany, and London all crashed, triggering circuit breaker rules that suspended trading in the darkness of the American night. The ship of destruction finally sailed up the East River, on to Manhattan Island, and right down Wall Street.

Advisors tried to convince the president to preemptively close the markets. "No can do," he bristled with executive bravado. "The markets must open. Refusing to open is a sign of capitulation and surrender. America never surrenders!"

The professorial Federal Reserve chairman — his ever-whitening beard and ever-receding hairline making him look ever-the-more gnomish — loosened his tie and poured himself a drink at the 9:30 open. Perhaps the great sovereign ship would not sink, he hoped. The Fed had key-stroked hundreds of billions of dollars throughout the night and had managed to prop up the jittery futures markets. The expectation was that this could tame the animal spirits in time for the NYSE open. But all hope was dashed as the market sank nine percent at the opening bell.

"Fools! Don't they know they're killing us all?" The Fed chairman cried out as he gulped his breakfast bourbon. The Plunge Protection Team, the Fed's equivalent of Special Forces, stepped in and started buying which stabilized things for a few moments. Then a rumble thundered through the sovereign hull when word got out that the Chinese were not buying anything. The dollar immediately began a rapid decent against the yuan.

The floor traders started asking questions. "Who's buying up the Treasuries? Chase? Citi? Deutsche? RBS? Goldman? Dubai? What did you say? Come again? You mean they all stopped trading Treasuries a week ago? Holy shit! Who, then? Direct dealers? Like who? Moriah LLC? Who the hell is that? You say they bought fifteen billion? Really? Some outfit called Crazy Horse bought ten? Who are they? I've never heard of them. What's going on? Where are the big banks? Wait a sec, this isn't right. Just heard two hedge funds liquidated due to redemptions. Are you sure about that? Oh My God! This is it! This is it! Abandon ship! Abandon ship! Get out now! Sell it all! Sell it to those pension fund chumps! Sell it all to the Fed before they stop buying. Sell! Sell! Sell! Sell! Sell!"

A full-fledged avalanche of panic ensued, cracking the hull of the multi-trillion dollar sovereign vessel. The unsinkable U.S.S. — United States Sovereign — Titanic sank, in a spectacular, cascading selloff with three-times record volume.

The Gnome downed his drink and poured another, and another, and watched the bond ticker on his closed circuit network. Prices down...4%...11%...18%.... Interest rates up plus .5%...plus 2.0%...plus 5.0%!

The Fed tried to pump out as much of the tsunami of debt as it could by key-stroking the hundreds of billions of dollars necessary to clear all the offers. The Plunge Protection Team went all in. They hijacked the fiber-optic bandwidth to make sure their buy orders got through first.   Then they stalled the private sellers. They worked covertly through friendly foreign central banks: the Bank of England, the Bank of Australia, the Banco de Panama — yeah that's right, Panama. They had private banks on the dole, too — not the household Wall Street names but most of the regional outfits. The Fed gave them huge guarantees and unlimited lines of credit and agreements to repurchase everything they bought. But the rumors of the Fed's scheme had gotten out. As the Fed key-stroked more and more dollars, and the names of the buyers of Treasuries got more and more obscure, and the purchase amounts got more and more spectacular, the dollar itself listed, then tipped over, then began sinking faster than the Treasuries they were supposed to be backed by.

The unsinkable Titanic of American sovereign debt, the flagship of profligacy and arrogance, was sucked into a vortex. Over the course of twelve hours, the dollar price of a Japanese car, a barrel of Saudi oil, and a container ship full of Chinese tchotchkes DOUBLED. The U.S. stock market big boys all tanked as the cost of rolling over their debt exploded. The exchanges plummeted further, going limit down and suspended trading in dollars.

The Gnome had seen enough. He stepped in and pulled the plug at 10:01. International currency exchange in dollars was suspended worldwide. Wire and ACH transfers were suspended. To prevent capital flight, transfers from checking and savings accounts to foreign banks were limited to one thousand dollars. Banks on the east coast opened for an hour so the patrician class from Martha's Vinyard could withdraw some walking-around money. Then all the banks went on a holiday. There was a flurry of internet activity as intrepid nerds tried to move their offshore money market dollars and PayPal accounts into foreign currencies and commodity money and Bitcoins, but that too was brought to a screeching halt when the internet kill switch was thrown on financial transactions.

At the silent, somber floor of the NYSE, the highlights of the president's speech played on yet another Chinese-made big screen above the ticker which read "U.S. Markets Closed...FOMC in emergency session...Yankees beat the Red Sox 4-2." The remaining traders on the floor erupted in sarcastic applause.

Vaughn took a moment before leaving for work to look in on his young daughter. He quietly pushed her door open and snuck into her room. She was still asleep, lying sideways in her crib with one tiny foot dangling out, buried in an avalanche of blankets and her monkey. Her cherubic cheeks moved slightly as she suckled blissfully on her pacifier. Vaughn felt she was getting a little old for pacifiers. A feeling swept over him as he watched her, like a breeze of fresh cool air in some stale, stagnant chamber. It was a righteous feeling, a sensation of clarity and purpose. *How bad will things get? What will I have to do for my family? What am I capable of doing?* The answers blew into him as he looked down at little Brooke.

With the country crumbling into talc under the weight of its hubris and corruption, with the Nero president blustering away with his platitudes, with the zombie masses taking their opiate of big media propaganda, Vaughn realized then and there that there would be nothing, no one, no event that would come between him and his family. He loved them more than his own life. He would pay any price for them. He found casting off that worry to be liberating. He released the millstone of worry that had been chained to him.

The dying Republic, a victim of its pointless, bankrupting wars, its corporate welfare and bloated nanny-state, finally succumbed. Her citizenry concerned themselves only with who was going to win American Idol. America was meaningless to Vaughn now. Now it was time for survival.

He felt an arm slip under his elbow and around his chest. It was Jess. She pulled in tight against him and rested her head between his shoulder blades.

"You were right," she whispered.

Her acknowledgement meant everything to him. He needed to be and do right by her and her assessment was the only one that really mattered. He was vindicated for dragging his family out to the store in the middle of the night. He almost took pleasure in seeing things unravel the way that they had, but he knew that that was selfish and foolish to think about things that way. He wondered if the karma wheel would spin back onto him somehow. Tough times were ahead for all.

Chapter 10

Mae would have preferred a better hotel, but the Airport Hyatt was boarded up. She couldn't bring herself to go back to the bunker, but she hadn't quite convinced herself to impose upon the only person she could in the whole of the greater Denver area. So she stalled, passing the dull nights with her security detail, turning them into lounge drinking buddies and ultimately one drunken and regrettable three-way.

Mae spent two weeks at the airport Red Roof Inn, waffling over what to do. She finally received the dreaded phone call. The voice was unfamiliar and nasal. *Some low-level Secret Service nobody,* she guessed. The voice informed her that her time at the hotel purgatory was up. She either had to go to the DIA bunker or find her own arrangements. She requested a driver and within the hour, a solitary black SUV limo picked her up.

"People will think I'm a senator or something, riding around in this thing," she joked as the limo rolled down the sparsely developed airport superhighway.

"Sorry, Ma'am. It's the only car we had with bulletproof glass," explained the driver.

They rolled down the pristine highway, which traversed property owned by one of the cronies who had secured the airport's funding and ensured Denver International Airport's terribly inconvenient location. Pena Boulevard spanned fifteen miles of bleak, windswept steppe, linking Interstate 70 to the gleaming, canvas spires of the most expensive airport ever built. Those spires rose up from the flaxen plain much like the pyramids, but the design was probably inspired more by that goofy artist Christo than by any grand ancient Egyptian stimulus project. Christo's prior art included hanging a humungous white curtain across a Colorado canyon in the 1970s.

Mae was relieved when they passed Bluecifer, a giant, blue, demonic horse sculpture with orange glowing eyes and the grim karma of having fallen over and killing its sculptor during its creation. Bluecifer was the symbolic gatekeeper for Denver International, and once past it, Mae hoped to have nothing more to do with that place. The entire complex felt sinister to her with its cryptic Masonic symbols and creepy murals of Armageddon. She also hoped to never see the two young men of her security detail again. She was making her getaway from all of it. She could not be persuaded to go back and pass through the red door and enter the airport bunker.

Traffic on I70 was very light that morning, as it had been for several days. The big economic crash was like a concussion bomb that scattered all the civilian agents of commerce. To make matters worse, the reeling banks had closed a half dozen times since that black Friday. On any given trading day, the slightest rumor triggered panic redemptions and movement into commodities. This didn't sit too well with the bankers, so they leaned on the Fed Chairman who in turn leaned on Congress to make the new alternative currencies less attractive than their dying dollar. The Currency Stabilization Act, drafted by the bankers themselves, rammed through by Speaker Leatherface, and hastily passed by Congress who had not been given time to read it, slapped a ninety percent windfall gains tax on the sale of twenty-five different commodities. But this didn't accomplish anything other than to drive the commodity markets out from the light of the exchanges and into the dark alleys of the black market. The SEC and IRS couldn't do much to enforce the new regulation, but at least government could say it was doing something. Government always has to do something. Things never change in that regard.

The first bank holiday was the longest at five business days and a weekend. By business day three, tens of millions of Americans had exhausted their emergency stores of frozen pizzas and soft drinks. Their diapers had all run out and so had their baby formula and then the graham crackers and the egg noodles and eventually even the olives and mustard.

In order to save everyone, FEMA set up egg noodle and baby formula distribution centers at all the nation's football stadiums. They were quickly inundated by angry, hungry, desperate mobs. The cops drove them back with their megaphones. The mobs regrouped. They were driven back again by water cannon and sound blasters. They re-formed. Out came the batons and the pepper spray. They finally dispersed for good.

Batons and pepper spray worked well for subduing the desperate mobs at the FEMA centers, but not so well at the banks where the throng had justice and retribution on their mind rather than hunger. Many banking institutions were set ablaze, often with their pitiable, essentially blameless, minimum-wage-earning clerks still holed up inside.

By the fourth business day of the holiday, many cops had been on duty for stretches of twenty-four straight hours. Their nerves and sanity were pushed beyond mortal limits. They had become, to borrow a Roger Waters analogy, the "rusty wire holding the cork that keeps the anger in". Not all of them held it in. Rumors of mass shootings both by and of cops swirled around on what was left of the internet. Television and the papers reported nothing of it. They didn't want to foment panic in Mainstream America.

Fearing an inability to prevent the cauldron of civil unrest from boiling over, the president took decisive action. He held a press conference flanked on either side by the Fed Chairman and T, the Treasury secretary — whose own red hair, small stature, and pointy nose gave him a leprechaun-like aura. So together The Gnome, The Leprechaun, and Prince Charming declared that the crisis was over and the banks would open and stay open for good the next morning. The fairy tale was to take place on a Friday, and the triumvirate clung to hope that they would only have to make it through one anxious day of holy-shit-this-might-be-our-last-chance-to-get-our-money-out mania. Then the establishment would be saved by the weekend.

Truckloads upon truckloads of paper money emerged from the garages of Federal Reserve regional banks. New bills were printed with bigger denominations of one thousand and five thousand dollars dubbed "Reagans" and "Roosevelts." To hell with catching the money-laundering drug dealers! America needed cash. The Fed stuffed the new bills into the vaults of every bank of any significance, nationwide.

The Fed chairman, the Treasury secretary and the president crossed their fingers and held their breath. Futures trading revealed nothing as the Plunge Protection Team was key-stroking money and buying everything in sight trying to tame the animal spirits once again.

Ding! Ding! Ding! Ding! Ding!

Their mouths dropped. In less than one hour the market reached its limit down again.

"Fuck!" exclaimed the president, flanked by his sidekicks in the Oval Office. He lit himself a Marlboro.

The trio somberly ordered the foreign currency trading desks closed again. No dollars were allowed to be dumped until the rulers could come up with some other scheme to halt the slide. The domestic banks, however, remained open. They had to. The entire economy had nearly seized with rigor mortis during a week without money.

As an emergency remediation, all the New York banks were given access to special lending facilities. In other words, every bank that the Fed Chairman had deemed too big to fail gained access to an unlimited line of credit, at zero percent interest, with principal that was never to come due, all in hopes that the big banks might churn enough digital dollars to survive the bank run.

The move to shutter the banks the week before proved disastrous. Keeping them open might have been even worse, but closing them definitely fomented a panic — giving it legs, as they say. The lesson of being caught without the ability to buy toilet paper because debit card transactions were shut off was not lost on Americans. Americans could be accused of sheep-like idiocy in times of plenty, but they were quick learners. They were not going to get devoured by the wolf again.

When word got out in the middle of the night that the banks were reopening, the lines quickly accumulated. When the doors opened, a swarm inundated the terrified bank tellers. The truckloads of cash were quickly exhausted despite personal withdrawal limits of ten "Reagans" per customer. Customers were turned away cursing. Some turned over the signs. Some banks reported assaults. Some were set on fire, again.

With their debit cards turned back on, there was a mad rush to the grocery stores and gas stations. People weren't buying potato chips and root beer, this time. Now they were buying fuel and canned goods and dried goods and paper products and batteries and medicine. The pumps and shelves were cleaned out in minutes. Americans indeed learned quickly.

The supply chain, a super complex machine greased by millions upon millions of credit transactions, began sputtering within hours of the initial collapse. Parts of it blew apart as unsound trucking companies ran out of gas and could not do anything about it other than have their drivers pull their trucks onto the shoulders and walk away.

But despite the gaping holes, sound businesses endured by the wits of their brilliant, industrious managers who hustled fuel with collateralized IOUs to keep their fleets rolling. The goods that were moving were moving based on million dollar deals sealed with handshakes and emails. There were crafty, resourceful men and women, millions of them, dealing in millions of products, making billions of decisions, holding what was left of the sputtering economic order together. They were adjusting to the extraordinary situation. They were surviving.

Then the government just had to do something again.

The government busybody administrators could not resist their pervasive and pathological urge to save the day and be heroes. So, like a monkey wrench—or more aptly a hand grenade—tossed into the machine-works, the busybodies went about meddling and destroying the fragile arrangements created by the resourceful business managers.

"How dare anyone profit in these extreme times!" the politicians declared. First, the evil price gougers were to be cited, then arrested. Then their assets were to be seized. This started with the gas stations and progressed to the sellers of produce, and then the merchants of diapers. The possibility of high profits, which could be made if one could get a truckload of diapers from New Jersey to Flagstaff, for example, was quickly doused by the government busybodies who made it illegal to make any exploitative windfall profits. The exploiters, who were on their way to Flagstaff to fulfill the desperate diaper demand and make a buck in the process, caught wind of the new regulations that could result in landing them in prison for five years. They turned their trucks around and went back home. The Arizonian babies were saved from those greedy capitalists. They would just have to do without diapers and the other things they needed, regardless of what their parents were willing to pay.

The government busybodies then decided that certain goods had to have priority. Priority was largely determined by political connection. The handlers of those goods were moved to the front of the growing fuel lines. This destroyed the complex procurement and hauling matrix of pickup, delivery and backhaul. Within hours of the regulation, trucks were rolling empty. Gluts and shortages of goods exploded everywhere. A mountain of tires accumulated in Toledo while trucks across the country were idled by flats.

Mae, of course, cared not one whit about any of it. She only studied econometrics and concepts like aggregate demand in her PhD program. She, like most quantitative economists, was incapable of comprehending the interdependent, infinite locus of goods and services and time preferences and personal choices that form the complex matrix of an economy. To her, like most modern PhDs, economics was just two intersecting curves on a graph and a bunch of equations with Greek letters. Besides, she was still getting paid. Her investments were being adjusted in value by keystroke entry so as to keep her whole.

Her job function as an assistant Treasury secretary was, for the moment, obsolete. The Asian countries were her clients and they were not speaking to anyone in the U.S. She had nothing to do except reach her hideout and wait until the whole thing blew over.

She gazed out the window from behind her Jackie-O sunglasses as her bulletproof limo flew down I70. The outside world had changed during the two weeks she spent inside the Red Roof Inn. She observed dozens of semi-trailers parked along the sides of the highway, their tires removed, their doors pried open, and their contents looted. Many were burned.

Several abandoned cars lined the interstate as well, mostly older models, beaten down by years of abuse, they finally gave out. They were the cars of poor people, older models, dented, and rusted. Their destitute owners lacked the wherewithal to get them home. All of these abandoned cars had their windows smashed, tires removed, and gas siphoned out. Whatever was of value on the inside was taken as well.

Mae sipped from a martini glass as they whizzed past the wreckage.

The interstates, the arteries of commerce spanning coast to coast, were becoming the repository of the plaque of economic collapse. Wasted vehicles on the roadside nearly outnumbered the vehicles still being driven on the road.

Mae's limo made good time until they hit a traffic jam.

"What's going on?" she asked, as she checked her lipstick in her compact. It had gotten smudged by her drink.

"Got a call out. Should hear any second," replied the driver.

"Well, I don't want to be stuck out here in Road Warrior land for long."

"Don't worry, Ma'am. We're bulletproof. And I can always call in air support, if necessary."

They sat there staring into the back end of a rusted out Sierra pickup, mud flaps emblazoned with chrome nude silhouettes. Its expired tag was from Guadalajara.

"Almighty says there was an explosion up ahead. DHS and FBI are on scene investigating. They think it was a roadside bomb. Can you believe that? An IED in Denver."

"How long is the wait?" Mae asked, impatiently.

"It could be a while, Ma'am."

"Any way we can take a detour?"

"Not from here. We're a half mile or so from the next exit."

Mae swallowed the last of her martini and dozed off in the air conditioned, leather seat.

Mae awoke to a forward lurch of the limo. She checked her watch. She'd been asleep for over an hour. They were still on I70 but at least they were moving. Mae poured another martini. After about twenty minutes of creeping along, the roadside carnage finally came into view. Two fire trucks, one facing the wrong direction, flanked the smoldering, burned-out car on the right lane of the elevated interstate. Its tires had completely burned away and the twisted, blackened heap of metal rested on its axles in a puddle of grease and fire retardant foam. A group of policemen were huddled on the shoulder. On the ground before them was a white sheet covering a bundle with two stumps of charcoal poking out one end. Mae took a giant gulp and sucked the olive off the plastic skewer.

"Never thought I'd see anything like that in America," remarked the driver who chomped away at his chewing gum as they passed the carnage.

"Surreal. It looks like a war zone."

"I'm afraid I've got some bad news, Ma'am."

"What's that?"

"We need to get some gas."

"Oh no, you're not stopping!" Mae ordered, now terrified at the prospect of pulling off the highway into some proletarian ghetto in a government limo.

"We're stopping one way or another, Ma'am."

"Then turn back," she ordered.

"Can't do it. We wouldn't make it half way back to DIA. Just relax. We'll be fine. Did I tell you we're bulletproof?"

"You did."

They pulled off the interstate onto an arterial and found an open gas station not far from the highway. Ahead of the pump was a long line of cars waiting for the petrol that had tripled in price in just three weeks. Mae's driver accelerated, bypassing them all, eventually angling the limo into the front of the line. The horns of the cars behind furiously let loose. Drivers started getting out of their cars and letting curses and gestures fly. "Who the hell are you?!" screamed a burly man with a mullet three cars back. He looked like he might stomp up and throw his hairy fist through the limo's bulletproof windshield, yank the driver out through the hole, and strangle him with his bare hands. The driver calmly radioed in the situation to "Almighty." Then, to Mae's surprise, he opened the door.

"Where're you going? Don't get out!" she screamed.

Mae's driver hopped out, spit out his gum and flashed his

badge to the cursing mob. "Everyone just calm down!"

The mob's response was a barrage of four-letter curses and threats of violence.

"I'm with the Federal Government," the driver continued as he raised his badge higher, as though it would give him more prestige. "I apologize for cutting into line like this but we must not be delayed. We are on official government business."

"Fuck you!" was the universal reply.

"The line starts back there," shouted mullet-man.

One car lurched forward and bumped the limo, jolting Mae's head back and spilling her martini down her chest. She was afraid.

"Everyone just calm down," the limo driver shouted. "It'll only be a minute and then we'll be on our way."

"You can wait in line just like everyone else," screamed a woman with a screaming kid strapped into her beat-up minivan.

"Look," the driver continued, "we are with the government. We are here to help you."

"Haven't you helped us enough?" asked the mullet-man. "Well, haven't ya? Move that damn car to the back of the line!"

The car that had just bumped Mae's limo backed up and revved its engine. Mae's driver apparently decided that the mob was neither impressed with his rank nor amenable to his reasoning, because he got back in and locked the door. Mae caught a glimpse of his concerned face in the rearview mirror. Images of the roasted car and the two charred stumps on the highway flashed through her mind. Her limo was bulletproof but it wasn't fireproof.

"Where are they?" shouted the driver into his radio.

"What's wrong with these idiots?" Mae interrupted. "Don't they know who we are?" Feeling the effects of the martini, she rolled down her window a few inches and screamed out at the mob, "Don't you imbeciles know who we are?"

One responded by tossing a bottle at her window which shattered into foamy shards on impact. Mae rolled the thick glass back up. "Let's get the hell out of here," she pleaded.

"Hang on. We've got air support coming."

"Then where the hell are they?"

Looking back, Mae noticed the mullet-man had produced an aluminum softball bat and was making his way to the limo. He stopped at each car along the way, cajoling the occupants to get out and join him. Many did. A gang of angry proles formed behind him as he approached.

"I hope they don't have anything flammable," said the limo driver.

"Let's go! Let's go now!" Mae shouted.

"Hang on. I hear them. They're coming."

"You're damn right they're coming. Get us out of here."

"No. The choppers. Listen."

The mullet-man reached the back of the limo. A posse of about a dozen had formed behind him. To Mae's surprise, her driver got out again.

"Don't be stupid!" he ordered the mullet-man. "Hear those choppers? Yeah. I called them. There coming here."

"Fuck you, Fed," the mullet-man man barked.

"I'm armed," the driver advised. "Don't make me use it."

"You can't shoot all of us."

"Yeah, that's true," the driver answered. "But I can shoot you. Then I can get back in this car and wait another two minutes for the cavalry to arrive and take out your posse. So I suggest you just calm yourself down and back away and I'll forget about how you threatened me with your deadly weapon. Threatening a government employee is a felony that carries a mandatory twenty-year prison term, you know. We'll just get our gas and be on our way."

The mullet-man looked ready to make his move. But he turned his head to look behind him and found that the others had gone back to their cars.

"Your odds aren't so good anymore," said the limo driver.

"Who do you think you are?" asked the mullet-man as he lowered his weapon.

"I'm with the government."

"You feds think you're royalty or something?"

"Want me to answer honestly?"

"No, I want you to lie to me some more," he replied sarcastically.

"Then yes. More or less, we are royalty. We're the government. Our job is to run things. And you're job is to do what you're told. It's for your own good."

"You're all liars. You caused all this. You destroyed the country."

"These are tough times, my friend. But we're all in it together."

"Yeah? Well some are 'in it' more than others."

A thumping black helicopter appeared over the surrounding cottonwoods and rooftops. It hovered around and above the limo. Mae glimpsed the sniper on board, taking aim. One gentle squeeze and the bullet would explode through the target's barrel chest, the energy of the .50 caliber round sending him flopping into the air like a tossed stuffed animal.

"Go back to your car," ordered the limo driver in a calm voice.

Chapter 11

"Will you do it?" asked Marzan.

"Do what? Shoot Americans?" asked Rollins as he screwed his Osiris eye ring down his middle finger.

Their unit had just received the situation report and rules of engagement in the back of their cramped Humvee. Nothing had really changed from how they were instructed back in Shariastan. The platoon was en route to a south Chicago ghetto to quell a developing situation. Rioters had amassed and were turning over cars, smashing out windows, and setting fires. The police had lost control.

Their orders were that rioters who did not disperse were to be given first a bullhorn warning, then tear gas, then a high-intensity sound blast, and finally warning shots. After that, the appropriate level of response was left to the discretion of the lieutenant, who in this case was a primped man-boy just out of officer candidate school. There was no objective other than to restore order. If they were fired upon, they were permitted to return fire...after headquarters approval, of course.

"Yeah, I mean shoot Americans," Marzan clarified.

"I guess I'm not really too worried about it," Rollins answered, nonchalantly. "I'm a soldier. Orders are orders. Does that surprise you?"

Marzan wasn't at all surprised. He probably shouldn't have asked him. He had known Rollins for eighteen months. He probably knew more about what Rollins was going to do than Rollins knew, himself.

Rollins never appeared to be concerned about what he was going to be doing. He operated reflexively by muscle memory. His complete moral detachment was well-established. If there was an order, Rollins would execute it without hesitation. Bulldoze somebody's house? Done. Lob a hand grenade into a courtyard? Done. Fire on a carload of *hajis* who failed to stop at a checkpoint? Done. No hesitation. No questions. Rollins carried out his orders as if he were playing a video game. There was never any remorse or second-guessing or empathy. He was nearly the perfect soldier.

I don't think I can do it, Marzan thought to himself, trying not to reveal his doubt to Rollins. He forced his face into a deadpan expression to hide any hint of his internal turmoil. He chided himself for not being as hard as Rollins. His conscience increasingly haunted him and he hated himself for it. He had to use the "remember your dead buddies" technique in order to clear his doubts.

I am weak and Rollins is strong, he thought. He was never comfortable with intimidating the *little brown people* like Rollins was. Despite their small stature and annoying, indecipherable babbling they called a language, Marzan could never fully dehumanize them. Their sad brown eyes would knife through his emotional armor. Through their eyes, he experienced their terror, grief, fear, submission, hatred.

He yearned to be Michael Rollins, encased in impervious emotional armor, impenetrable to any blade. He wanted to see only deception in the enemy's glances. He desperately wanted everything else — all that touchy-feely bullshit — deflected away. If he were only as hard as Michael Rollins he could be cured of the pain of conscience.

All *hajis* were liars and savages, much like all the *gooks* in Vietnam were liars and savages, and all the *Japs* and *krauts* during World War II were liars and savages. Things never change in war. The soldier is taught that he is the überman. The enemy is unhuman. In Shariastan, it was assumed that just as soon as the GI's back was turned, *haji* was sneaking off to his spider hole to finish improvising his explosives. All unhumans are of one savage, evil mind.

"Look," continued Rollins, "we're giving them plenty of warning. If they don't want to get themselves dead then they should do what they're told. It's pretty simple: Don't be a dumbass. Respect my authority. Respect this." Rollins jammed a magazine into his M4 and yanked the charging handle.

Marzan wondered why Rollins didn't return the question. *Is he really that self-absorbed?* he wondered. *Or did he sense my uneasiness about the matter and decide to let me off the hook? No way. He would never let me off the hook. He's definitely that self-absorbed,* he concluded.

Their Humvee stopped.

The night was illuminated by rippling gold dancing on the unsmashed window glass of the numerous store fronts down the street. The power was cut off intentionally to give the Domestic Security Force — or DSF, the new name for Marzan and Rollins's Division — a technological advantage. Cut the power and you greatly reduce enemy coordination and documentation. The U.S. Army loves to fight at night because the lightly armed, third-world insurgents they typically engage can't see. The Army also had to ensure the battery backups of the nearby cell towers were turned off as well. This was a bit of a pain in the ass, but it got done.

The troops dislodged themselves from their Humvees. They huddled for a moment to receive last-minute instructions and activate their night vision. Then they began their stealthy maneuver into the darkness with the Humvees crawling behind. Their viewfinders pictured green silhouettes scrambling between alleyways, aimlessly hurling bricks and Molotov cocktails.

"Dumbasses," Rollins whispered into the radio.

Marzan watched them scurry around in the darkness, oblivious to the laser sites that were marking them. *They would never expose themselves as stupidly as this in Shariastan,"* he thought as he moved his laser dot from target to target. The Shariastan insurgents learned quickly that the night provides no cover against U.S. Army night vision. But they learned that being still and covering up in wool blankets does.

The soldiers progressed slowly, deliberately, knees bent, rifles aimed, and targets acquired and reacquired. They proceeded around a corner and a block down the street, past the Carniceria, past the prepaid cell-phone store that served the neighborhood drug dealers, up to the Checks Cashed façade at the corner. The firelight danced in flickering green in their optics. Marzan could hear glass smashing and the primordial, raging laughter of an insanity-fueled mob.

What is their problem? Marzan asked himself.

The proles were angry about prices. They were angry about shortages. They were angry about joblessness. They were angry that their welfare checks were delayed. They were angry about being hungry. They were angry that mass transit had stopped servicing their area. They felt trapped. They had been lied to. They had never known an instant in their life when some government bureaucrat wasn't telling them what to do, where to go, or giving them the financial means to do it. Now their government benefactors were pulling away, disconnecting from them, cutting them off. Despair and panic had set in.

Terrified and not knowing what to do, they gathered and protested during the daylight hours. The cops rode in — polyester vials of mustachioed nitroglycerine. Their nerves were worn thin by twenty-four-hour shifts. They were being asked to do many exceptionally dangerous things that they did not sign on to do.

Someone hurled a brick that careened off a cruiser windshield, shattering it. The cops drew their pistols. Most of the rioters scattered but the angriest among them, the unattached, the unemployed, the unencumbered young men remained. They hurled rocks and bottles and taunts at the cops. A cop was hit in the chest with half a cinderblock.

Gunfire!

No one other than the actual shooter knew who fired first. The cops returned fire with a barrage of 9mm rounds. It sounded like Chinese New Year. Then screams. A wild murmuration of young men ran this way and that. More shots. Someone was firing back with a rifle. More screams.

Outnumbered a hundred to one, the cops retreated back into their cruisers. The mob enveloped them. Fearing a rout, the cops withdrew. A Pyrrhic victory riot ensued.

Marzan was the first to peek around the corner at the rioters. The mob was much bigger than he had anticipated. There were hundreds. The fire teams took their positions. A Humvee pulled into the street and with an enormous bullhorn affixed to its roof it addressed the crowd.

"You are hereby ordered to disperse!"

Rollins laughed as he sighted on one of the "dumbasses," as he called them. The target was some fifty yards off. These idiots got no idea what's coming." Rollins said. "You better get the hell out of here before the U.S. Army smokes your ass."

The firelight flickered in the bulletproof windows of the Humvees, casting a surreal omen. Some rioters spotted the soldiers and their M4s and took cover. Others fled, sensing something wicked was about to happen.

The sight of cops might be cause for concern to the rioters, but cops, although locally despised, were local scoundrels who lived locally and had to answer to locals for what they did. This time, the proles were staring into the ranks of heavily-armed soldiers...mercenaries by all accounts. These soldiers were from faraway places like Orange County and Philadelphia and Houston. They might as well have been foreign invaders from China, as far as the rioters were concerned. These mercenaries had no connection or affiliation to that south-Chicago neighborhood. The soldiers, by and large, deemed the neighborhood as just another foreign battlefield — as if it had been chiseled out of a Shariastan desert and plopped right down into Illinois.

The rioters that did not flee held their concept of being an American before them. They cradled that abstract notion, contemplating it, trying to decide if it was real or just some sort of vaporous nonsense drilled into their brains by public school, national holidays, and television.

The tear gas was launched.

Fearlessly, some rioters grabbed the smoking canisters and tossed them back. The big show of authoritarian force is always just that, a show. There would be some back and forth, the mob would blow off a little steam, then the storm troopers would march in and methodically disperse the crowd. That's the way it always works during riots.

The sound-blaster sirens blared.

They wailed so loud that it made teeth chatter. A few brittle windows crumbled under the pulsating noise. The rioters scattered into the alley ways and behind burned out cars to shield their ear drums.

Warning shots were fired.

It was at that moment that the rioter's remaining notions of being an American dissolved. America had now just become some far-away gang of white politicians sending an army in to occupy their neighborhood. Only their homes and their friends and their families meant anything to them, from that moment on. They knew then that there wasn't going to be any theatrical, non-lethal dispersal.

Rifle shots came from a window somewhere above.

"Smoke 'em!" came the order from the lieutenant through the earpiece radios of the soldiers — after headquarters' approval, of course.

The Domestic Security Force opened fire in three round bursts. Muzzle flash. Ricochet. Beelike-buzzing zips of bullets sliced the air. Dull clangs resonated as automobile hulls were punctured by the rounds.

Rollins gently squeezed his trigger. The victim did a full cartwheel before landing on his face, the American dying in no more special manner than any other of the several dozen little brown people Rollins had already smoked.

After ten more seconds — which seemed like forty-five minutes to the outmatched, outgunned and terrified rioters — the hail of gunfire ended.

The whooshing sound of flames.

Groans from the wounded.

Car alarms wailing.

The platoon advanced to check out their damage, now behind the cover of their lumbering Humvees. Rollins approached his victim with Marzan to his flank. It was a kid, maybe seventeen. He had run right out of one of his sneakers. "Funny how that weird stuff happens sometimes," Rollins remarked.

Chapter 12

Undersheriff Garrity had been working for twenty-five straight hours. He had reached the point of sleep deprivation where his mind began morphing things out of the shadows that darted across the highway in front of his SUV. He slapped his face back into consciousness.

The past two days had been without precedent. He received a call from an agent of the Department of Homeland Security who informed him that the agency would soon be coordinating (i.e. taking over) the county sheriff's department. Garrity would have a new boss and this new command structure would be in place for an indefinite period of time. The agent explained to him that the fderal takeover was being done for the sake of national security.

A black Yukon appeared at the station soon after the call and two young, well-groomed, sunglasses-wearing agents in blue suits set up shop in Garrity's office—at his desk, no less. They rudely brushed Garrity off, and at one point condescendingly asked him to go get them coffee. Garrity stormed out of his office. He deeply resented them.

An appeal to the sheriff was no use as his boss had a new federal master, too.

"You gotta do something. Get rid of these assholes," Garrity pleaded.

"What's wrong with you, Bob? Where's your sense of duty? Your patriotism?" asked the sheriff.

Garrity pondered quitting right then and there. It wasn't like they were paying him for his extra hours anyway. He was being issued scrip, as the county was in bankruptcy and insolvent. The new, fancy paper was worth even less than the old federal reserve notes, when and where it was accepted at all.

Garrity escaped into his cruiser and out onto patrol. He didn't answer the sheriff's or the fed's calls or bother to pick up their coffee. There was plenty of work for him to do maintaining community visibility and enforcing the nationwide midnight-to-dawn curfew, which essential government workers and portions of New York City, Boston and D.C. were exempted from.

It was two a.m. when Garrity reached the point where he could no longer stay awake. He had been working through a list of gun owners supplied from the background check databases, temporarily confiscating their rifles, pistols, and shotguns. No one seriously resisted, to his surprise, although some complained and threw that god damned piece of paper (aka The Constitution) in his face. Garrity just smiled at them, allowed them to vent for a moment, then conspicuously slid his hand down toward the taser clipped to his belt. This motion pacified all resistance.

Garrity was not surprised to find that neither Joe Joe nor any of his MS13 gangbanger buddies, nor any other known felons or persons-of-interest appeared on his gun registry. Felons couldn't legally own a gun, but everyone knew that they still had them. Garrity got a chuckle about that. A lot of good it does to confiscate guns when the only people who give them up are the law-abiding citizens.

He turned on the hair metal music channel on his taxpayer-funded, recently-bailed-out, satellite radio. The ballad "Every Rose Has Its Thorn" filled his cab. It was so familiar a song to Garrity that he thought it a chore to even listen to it. But when he felt himself starting to doze off, he rolled down the window, stepped on the gas, took a swig from his flask, and burst into verse.

"Though it's been a while now
I can still feel so much pain.
Like a knife that cuts you
The wound heals
But the scar, that scar remains."
Garrity took another swig and immersed himself in self-pity.
"Every rose has its — oh, fuck this!"

He switched the radio off and tuned in the frozen night air as it swooshed through the window. He looked down at the speedometer. He was doing eighty which was was double the speed limit on the winding canyon road. *No worries,* he thought. There wasn't a soul out save for him. His SUV bobbed and pitched as the road rippled and snaked down Ed's Hill. He slowed to make his turn, then floored it again as he straightened out on a dirt road. The wheels kicked up a swarm of stones and pebbles. Two more turns and he pulled into his garage.

Garrity got out and opened the back hatch. He stared excitedly at the neatly stacked cache of confiscated guns, contemplating adding one of them — an early 1900s double barrel shotgun — to his permanent, personal collection. *It'll look really sweet over my fireplace,* he thought. When or if it was ever supposed to be returned to its owner was anybody's guess. If it ever was, Garrity could merely deny any knowledge of it. The owner would go to the county clerk and file some grievance in triplicate, which would be ignored until the owner finally gave up in frustration. Citizens usually gave up on those sorts of things after about 90 days. The vintage gun was as good as his if his conscience would permit him to keep it.

Garrity heard his two German shepherds barking away inside. He opened the door into the house and patted their heads. "So sorry, sweeties." He made his way to the kitchen where he offered them some cheese. He watched them wolf it down in one gulp. "You dogs just can't grasp the idea of savoring, can you?"

Daisy and Himmelstoss were Garrity's family. He loved them as much as anything in the world. Daisy, an anachronistic name for a German shepherd, was the alpha female. She was always the first to bark and the first to greet. Himmelstoss, a male, was named after a WWI German war *hero* from some pussified anti-war book he never bothered to read in high school literature class. Himmelstoss was a bit clunky for a dog's name so he shortened it to "Stossi" which also sounded like a reference to East German secret police making it even keener in his mind. Daisy and Stossi had outside access through a doggy door so Garrity's long shifts did not result in accidents.

Garrity scooped out some dog food for them, but they were uninterested. "Oh, you guys just want the good stuff, eh?" He tossed them each another cube of cheese. He grabbed himself a beer from the fridge and made his way to the family room with his loyal dogs following behind. He fell into his leather sofa and flipped on the television. The big media talking heads materialized, giving calm reassurances to the masses.

"Hello, Bobby," came a velvety voice from the shadowy corner of the room.

Garrity spit out a gulp of Bud Light. His eyes swung to the side where he finally saw her. *She came back. I knew she would,* he thought. "What are you doing here?" he asked her, feigning indifference. "And why didn't my dogs rip you to pieces? Bad dogs!"

"There, there Daisy. Good boy, Stossi," she replied, stroking their heads when they came to her and sat at her feet. "They remember me, Bobby. Aren't you happy to see me?"

"What makes you think I want you here?" he said, trying to sound like he didn't care that she came back. "You should have called first."

"I wanted to surprise you. Tell me you're happy to see me." She got up and slithered over to him as the dogs watched from the floor with wagging tails. She took up the spot next to him on the sofa. "Bobby." She always purred his name when she wanted something. That simple trick always managed to knife in under his plates of emotional armor. He was defenseless to it. "It's been a long time, Bobby. I missed you." She slid her arm over his shoulders.

Garrity kept up the phony resistance the best he could. "What do you want, Mae? How'd you get here? Don't you have important government things to do these days? Isn't there some French banker you should be having dinner with tonight?"

"Oh Bobby, don't be crude," she said. "I came here to see you."

"You think I believe that? That you came out here just to see me? What do you take me for, Mae? Just tell me what you want."

"It's crazy out there, Bobby," Mae continued, shifting from seduction to supplication. "I had nowhere to go. They wouldn't fly me back to D.C. and they wouldn't pay for my hotel. They wanted us to stay in some dungeon at Denver International. I couldn't stay there. That place is awful. I kept thinking of you, how close you are. You're the only one I could turn to. Won't you help me?"

Garrity pretended to look irritated, but inside he was elated to see his ex-wife. She had left him two years before when she got her Treasury Department gig. Lured by world travel, prestige, a fat salary, and the chance to hobnob with the most powerful men in the world, she ditched her provincial, redneck cop husband. He was not a suitable escort in the spheres of geopolitical power.

Bobby tried to hold his illusion of resistance together.

"Do you have any money?" he asked.

"Huh? Oh no, nothing but scrip and this government debit card."

"You can't buy anything with those. We go shop to shop making sure the stores take them but as soon as word gets out that a store's taking scrip, their shelves get cleaned out."

"So how do people get by?"

"They eat a lot of cornbread and cheese and wait in lines, I guess. Some barter. People survive, that's what they do. I get to eat at the department and commandeer gas. I even get dog food rations cuz I got Daisy and Stossi rated as police dogs."

Mae started caressing Garrity's forearm. "Bobby..."

"What?" he asked, refusing to make eye contact with her.

"Let me stay with you a little while. I feel safe with you."

"I don't know. I don't think I can provide you the royal lifestyle you're accustomed too."

"Don't be cruel, Bobby. I could go stay in that dungeon if it were necessary, but I'd rather be here with you. I know how tough things were between us. But when I was all alone, my perspective changed. I realized I was wrong. I know that now. Just give me a chance. I need you, Bobby."

She massaged his shoulder and the gears in Garrity's brain started to turn. She had him and he knew that she knew it. He knew that she could just reappear at any moment in his life and that would be enough. She was irresistible to him. *I'm weak,* Garrity thought.

For him, it was as if his prayers had been answered—answered with a curse. He was already plotting in his mind how to extract repayment from her and to what level of depravity he might be able to extract it. Mae never had any intimate boundaries.

When their marriage was dissolving, Garrity rationalized that it was probably the toll of stress that paved the way for their separation. But this was a spectacular stroke of good fortune and perhaps a final opportunity to redeem himself and recapture the woman who was the only obsession in his life. He wished he had been working out and eating healthier. He was disgusted with his appearance. But the gears kept turning in his mind.

"We gotta get out of here," he said.

"What do you mean?"

"I don't know, away from here. Out of the country for a while. Some place warm. Mexico. Costa Rica. At least until things settle down."

"How much money do we need for that?"

"A lot."

"How will we get it, Bobby?" she asked, wrapping her other arm around him, squeezing his chest and pressing her breasts against him. He surrendered, totally dropping the façade of resistance with the sensation of her firm curves and her warm, smooth skin beneath her clothes. She placed her right leg over his lap. He caught himself breathing a little loud. The gears in his brain seized.

"I have an idea."

"I knew you would, Bobby," she answered as she pulled back. She got herself up and sauntered into the kitchen. "That's why I loved you."

Chapter 13

"It's over," explained Vaughn's boss with averted eyes. He wore a look of surrender on his face. "We didn't get the federal contract so we're shutting it down. There's nothing more we can do."

Vaughn wasn't surprised. He had seen the books. Costs for fuel and insurance were soaring and the customer base was dissolving like a sand castle in the tide. And the customers that remained weren't paying timely, so they might as well have been swept away as well. Without the contract, it didn't take a CPA to see the inevitable.

"Who got the deal?"

"Reznick."

"Reznick's not minority-owned is it?"

"No, but he's a big donor. I suppose that's how it works now. It's all politics. Here's your deposit stub. I'm sorry, Vaughn. I appreciate all you've done for me these years. I wish I could do more."

"I understand," Vaughn replied.

"I hope you can get your money out and buy what you need before the banks close again."

They shook hands.

Vaughn went to his desk and began packing up his things. A lot of stuff can accumulate in ten years, even in a small space. It took him three trips to get it all out of his cubicle and into his truck.

He stopped to survey the deserted parking lot on his final trip. His firm was one of the last ones hanging on in the office park. A massive "For Sale - Bank Owned" sign decorated the entrance. But despite the building's inspirational architecture, manicured lawns, and its green construction rating—which meant that its low-flush-volume toilets required three flushes—no prospective renters had called on the property in eight months.

Vaughn sighed, got in his truck and started up the engine, praying he had enough gas to get home. Before putting it in gear, he looked down at the box he had set on the passenger seat. On top of the stash of file folders and fading documents was a photo of his wife and daughter holding a kite string and looking upwards into the sky. Those were such hopeful times.

The family had some savings but not enough to get them through the winter. Vaughn was going to have to find something, and what a horrible time it would be looking for work. The only people who had jobs seemed to be people working for the government. *Fat chance getting one of those gigs,* he thought. Vaughn called the government workers "tax feeders." They seemed to be carrying on as if nothing was happening to the economy at all. Vaughn decided that if he saw one of them protesting a government wage freeze or pension reduction, he would run him down right then and there. No, not really, but it felt good to channel his rage. *You can't really blame them,* he thought. *They just want to take care of their families. They're no different from me.*

Vaughn felt burdened. *Will we lose the house?* There was a 180-day moratorium on foreclosures enacted by executive order. There seemed to be a new executive order every day. The bankers holding delinquent mortgages were placated by a relaxation in accounting rules and another round of congressionally approved bailouts on the order of another trillion dollars. *A trillion here, a trillion there...pretty soon they will be talking about some real money,* Vaughn joked to himself. *How many trillions was it up to now? Who knows? At least we'll have a place to stay for a while. That's a positive.*

Vaughn pulled out of the parking space. *Am I a failure?* he asked himself as he drove out of the empty lot. *Define 'failure,'* he answered himself. *Define it in today's context. I suppose being unable to feed and shelter my family would constitute failure. We're not there yet. Besides, nobody starves to death in America. If worse came to worst, we could always move in with my mother.* Vaughn chuckled at the thought of Jess and his mother living together under one roof. *This'll all blow over. Even if we lose everything, I'll get it all back once things recover. Believe in yourself, Vaughn Clayton. Don't worry.*

He drove past the "For Sale" sign noticing it had been tagged with an image of a sickle and hammer. The idea that it would be his final time driving out of that lot affected him with a disorienting feeling of loss. The last time he had experienced such a sensation was at high school graduation when the realization that a door was permanently closing on a phase of life. It seemed so significant at that time. Now he felt a mixture of sadness, hopelessness, cynicism, and fear. But he also felt relief and liberation. He didn't know if he wanted to sob, celebrate, or smash something. He had worked so hard there only for it all to be for naught. *You are always taught that if you work hard and persevere you will succeed,* Vaughn thought. He wasn't so sure if that axiom held anymore. Resourcefulness and craftiness probably had more to do with success than hard work these days.

Vaughn passed at least twelve police cruisers on his thirty-mile commute home. He also passed police Humvees and police MRAPS and even a police tank. He didn't imagine they were catching speeders with these newly commissioned armored vehicles.

As Vaughn approached the outer beltway, he took special note of the strip malls and office buildings that lined the route he had traversed for years. The architecture of the buildings was familiar, like landforms to a sailor making an inland passage, but he examined the details on this particular drive. He looked into the windows. So many were closed, empty, or boarded up. More than half, he guessed. He looked at their walls, covered in graffiti. He noticed the sickle and hammer, again, and again. "The grocery stores," he muttered. "Grocery stores never go out of business. Everyone has to eat." Yet there they were, or at least their abandoned husks. Vaughn counted four empty grocery stores along the way.

He whizzed past apartments and condominiums advertising free rent for three months. Many were empty, abandoned. Some had their windows and facades blackened by fire and left that way. *Where did all the people go?* he wondered. He took note of the numbers of abandoned houses with their unkempt yards, broken windows and vacant driveways. *So many empty houses. Who is going to buy them all? Why did they build so many in the first place? Who made the loans for their construction? Who made out those mortgages? Where did all the damn money come from? Where did it all go?*

His needle was on "E." The trip home was going to cut it close.

He searched for an open gas station. None were to be found as even the gas stations were dying. Three and fourfold increases in prices couldn't save them. The convenience stores and the fast food joints — they never closed fast food joints — were disappearing. Golden arch rainbows ended at a big pot of boarded-up emptiness. So many were gone. Some were even bulldozed, leaving nothing but scarred earth, which was overrun by noxious thistle weed. Nothing overran the thistle. Some shops were fortunate enough to be reborn as dog groomers and prepaid cell phone outlets, only to die again. *This didn't happen overnight,* he thought. *It's been dying for years.*

There was one sector of the economy that was still thriving, though: the banks. The banks and their big, blocky, menacing, obnoxious buildings were all still brimming with activity. These survivors were not the puny local banks and credit unions, mind you, but the big, bloated, behemoth national banks. Banks with patriotic, bankerly names like Ameribank, Freedombank, Libertybank, National,

U.S., Allied, Republic, and Victory. Their names sounded as if they were devised by Roosevelt's war propagandists. They all remained intact and gleaming, with their buff-polished granite, their plush lawns neatly groomed, their hedges sculpted into fluffy green balls, and fresh stripes of luminescent gold lining their smooth, black parking lot asphalt. Their lots were full, too, corralling the jalopies of their employee wage-serfs. These hourlies were charged with determining the creditworthiness of human borrowers by a ten-question computer algorithm. No skill at character evaluation was needed. No need for business modeling and what-if analysis. No need to even look them in the eye. Customer relationships? Far too extravagant an expense. A spreadsheet and a regression equation can replace a professional human. Any monkey can press ten buttons. What if the equations are wrong and the loans go bad? Who cares? These banks are too big to fail. Welcome to the MegaBank team. Here, put on this blue polo shirt and nametag and stand over there.

Everyone was warned by media talking heads time and time again, "If the banks fail, the economy will collapse, and then America will regress into a third-world country like Haiti." Americans believed it. So the banks were infused with trillions of bailout dollars and their worthless assets were bundled up and delivered unto the banker's bank—the *uber*-bank—the mother of all banks, the Federal Reserve. There was no need to worry about taking on risk. The Fed is god! It can print the money necessary to keep all the banks going and going and going. A trillion. Two trillion. Four. Eight. Sixteen trillion. They would double down after each crisis. Anything less than that and the Ponzi scheme would collapse.

And while the Fed presented its teat to its banker cronies, the rest of the economy starved and withered away. The bankers prospered on rackets like Fed-backed investments that would not be allowed to lose money, and the carry-trade which involves printing money, loaning it to the banks at zero percent interest, and then the banks loaning it out to stock brokers at plus-two points. The banks paid multi-billion-dollar bonuses to their Manhattan executives while the auto lots and the grocery stores and the restaurants and the apartment complexes and the carpet cleaning businesses and the construction firms and the manufacturing plants died. The Wall Street banksters took it all for themselves. The chumps on Main Street, the ones who were told by big media talking heads that it was still indeed a "free market," starved to death awaiting a computer algorithm's approval of their lines of credit.

Yeah, it sure was a good thing that the banks were bailed out. If they weren't, America would have turned into a third-world country! Vaughn laughed at that irony as he scanned the economic ruin and the broken-down, burning cars and the cops driving around in tanks and the piles of litter and tires and busted furniture and soda bottles filled with urine that collected on the shoulder of the highway.

His needle was now below 'E.'

Vaughn wondered why he didn't notice it all before. He supposed he was always dimly aware of it but he never really processed it. "But why? It didn't happen overnight. I guess it took losing a job to wake up to it. It's a recession when a neighbor loses his job. It's a depression when you lose yours," he mumbled.

The government, on the other hand, was doing its best to redirect the boiling domestic rage. For months, they presented a financial scapegoat through their proxies in the media. "Those evil, sneaky Asians! How dare they dump America's Treasury debt and crash our dollar! It's an act of war! We must retaliate! We want tariffs! We need to teach them a lesson!" The media, of course, never used bigoted terms like "evil" and "sneaky" directly. The media were all college-educated, East Coast progressives who would never permit themselves to even be accused of a proletarian gutter trait like racism. But that was exactly what the message was. Every story used code words like "unexpected" (i.e. sneaky) and "destructive intent" (i.e. evil). The language filled the American minds with scary imagery. "Don't the Japanese know they are killing themselves?" asked the commentators, invoking images of kamikaze pilots crashing into American battleships.

The media read their politically-correct scripts while file footage played of Mao and Buddhist monks and Asian men dressed in western suits bowed to each other. The narrative was that China and Japan, two nations that have hated each other for a thousand years, were all of the sudden new best friends conspiring against America. It was all very subtle, designed to allow the media to maintain their aura of self-righteousness while deflecting American rage away from the real culprits.

The jingoist campaign was very effective at stirring up and distracting the American proletariat. The economic war fever spread like a plague delivered by fleas on supersonic flying rats. The Chinese and Japanese, who were merely protecting themselves, as any self-interested rational people would, were dehumanized by the American press.

Vaughn drove up into the foothills. His morning commute in to

91

work was brightened by sunshine, but the premature drive home was clouding over. There was a hint of snow as specs of white danced over his hood.

The needle went back up to "E" as his truck climbed and his gas tank inclined.

He turned on the radio.

"Unpatriotic short sellers are pushing the equity markets down as — "

He flipped to the next station.

"Reports indicate heavy casualties as the 101st attempts to break out from encirclement. This marks the first time since the Korean War that American forces have been — "

Next station.

"Greedy speculators drive the price of oil up to a record high for a twenty-second consecutive trading day. The Secretary of State is meeting with OPEC officials to work out the details of — "

Next station.

"In order to combat the persistent disinformation undermining law enforcement and security efforts, the president is issuing a signing statement to attach provisions to the Cyber Security Act that enables the Department of Homeland Security to block malicious, unpatriotic websites..."

Flashers just ahead. Checkpoint. Checkpoints had become commonplace. Vaughn slowed and stopped. The officer approached. Vaughn rolled down his window.

"Where're you headed?" the cop asked authoritatively, sunglasses reflecting the sunless gray sky.

"Home."

"And where's home?"

Vaughn gave him his address.

"License, please," the cop asked.

Vaughn handed it over. The cop scanned it into his database, gave it back, and waived Vaughn through.

Vaughn passed the last gas station and turned off the highway onto the winding canyon road leading up to his neighborhood. The silent, ancient ponderosa pine filled the view through the windshield. Nobody was on the road at that time of day. It was a workday, after all, and those that had jobs were at them and those that didn't were on the internet pretending to look for one. Vaughn turned onto his lane. Dogs came out to bark at him as he passed. Snowflakes danced in the air. He turned the last bend in the road and approached his driveway.

Something wasn't right. He couldn't put his finger on it at that instant but something was out of place. *An open window. A strange car? No. What then?* Then he saw it. It was an unusual tire rut in the muddy shoulder leading to the top of his driveway. He stopped his truck and examined it, trying to comprehend where it might have come from. *A delivery truck?* He couldn't think of what Jess would have had delivered.

He pulled into his long driveway and stopped at the front of the house. The front door was wide open. Something was definitely wrong. It was below freezing. The wind was starting to really whip the snowflakes around. He parked and jogged up to the door. He could hear his daughter screaming. He entered the house. He gasped. The house was in shambles. The furniture was turned over. The cupboards were thrown open. Piles of smashed dishes and picture glass and lamps and books and papers and overturned potted plants littered the floor.

He rushed into his daughter's room. Brooke was standing up in her crib with a crimson, contorted, screaming little face. Vaughn shouted for Jessica. There was no answer. He picked up the toddler and darted from room to room. "Jessica!" Still no answer. Brooke's screams turned to sobs as she plunged two fingers into her mouth. Vaughn found the bedroom ripped apart. The mattress was turned over and cut open There were chunks of foam exploded everywhere. The contents of the closet were strewn across the floor. The carpet in the corners was ripped up, revealing the plywood subfloor. He dialed Jessica on his cell. It rang. He bounced Brooke up and down to calm her sobbing. It rang. Brooke clutched tightly. It went to voicemail.

"Where are you!" he shouted into the phone.

Brooke started screaming again, startled by his tone.

Vaughn sat down with her and calmed her again by holding her head on his shoulder and rocking gently. He looked out the window at the snow that was beginning to accumulate on the pines outside. The magpies were fleeing to their nests.

Both doors into the house were still open and a bitter cold draft blew through the house from one end to the other. Vaughn rocked little Brooke. Brooke's tiny hands were purple and cold. He carried her to each door, kicked the debris out of the way to clear a path, and closed them.

"What is happening?" he asked.

He sat down again and took a deep breath. His heart was pounding. He had difficulty getting enough air. His mind sifted through all the details trying to cobble them together into something coherent. There was no possible explanation for events other than something horrible.

Pounding, pounding, pounding heartbeats.

"Breathe," he commanded.

Chapter 14

It was a whirlwind tour for Marzan and Rollins. First Chicago, then Houston, Atlanta, back to Chicago, then Detroit, St. Louis and many places in between. They tear gassed rioters and fired on looters one day, then handed out bottled water and freeze-dried chicken nuggets to serfs the next. At least it said it was chicken on the foil packets with the blue eagle emblems on them.

The market supply chain had disintegrated under the fivefold increase in fuel prices. Few stores could sell anything profitably. The market sclerosis, induced by the interventions of the meddling bureaucrats, finally forced the federal government to take *really* drastic action. The Food and Agriculture Price Stabilization Act, FAPSA for short, was drafted by a consortium of Big Ag corporations, passed by Congress in the dead of night, and signed into law by the president eight days after it was written.

"Never let a good emergency go to waste." as they say.

Partnering with enforcement from the USDA, the FDA and the ATF, FAPSA established compacts and exchanges — which were to be run exclusively by Big Ag, of course — through which all the nation's foodstuffs were required to pass. The Big Ag executives were going to get filthy, filthy rich. The enabling congressmen got massive donations. The family farmers, who sold their eggs and milk and beef off the newly licensed exchanges, were to be arrested and jailed.

The day after they left St. Louis, Marzan and Rollins bulldozed two farm houses with a camouflaged army bulldozer. Then they gathered all the milk from several dairy farms and poured it down the sewer. The next morning, they euthanized a poultry farm's chickens with flame throwers and tossed them into a hole. All this because those farmers violated the new FAPSA regulations in one manner or another. That afternoon, Marzan and Jimmy found themselves handing out chicken rations, again. Then they dispersed those very same serfs with tear gas and warning shots when they protested later that night.

"Ungrateful dumbasses," Rollins remarked.

Marzan was growing ill about everything. Every time he hopped out of his Humvee and into some farm or trailer park or urban ghetto he would get nauseous. He had missed all his targets intentionally, but this also filled him with guilt. He felt he was letting down his band of brothers by his subversive actions, but he simply could not bring himself to shoot at Americans.

Marzan was growing numb to the ceaseless Army jingoism. The sergeant would decry the "evil Docoms" — Domestic Combatants — while beating his chest like an ape. "They are NOT Americans," he would scream. "They are insurgents! They are terrorists! Smoke 'em!" The sergeant was skilled at dehumanizing the enemy. Operational effectiveness required his mercenaries to forget they were in America. They were still in a Shariastan, only with Wal Marts.

Jimmy Marzan was walking the edge of a razor, balancing the demands of a soulless mercenary with the conscience of a poet warrior. He recalled taking an oath at his induction to uphold the Constitution. He was no longer sure if that meant anything. It was getting difficult to reconcile the idea that he had to invade and occupy and oppress Americans in order to defend American freedom. The more he thought about that paradox, the less inclined he was to believe that he had ever actually defended any American's freedom. *Smoking all those little brown people didn't seem to benefit anyone,* he thought, *Unless you count the money the defense contractors made on the whole bloody enterprise.*

The longer Jimmy balanced on that razor the deeper it cut. He prayed every day that things would settle down before he fell over to one side or the other. But it had been two months since that first Chicago riot and the chaos seemed only to be getting worse.

Michael Rollins appeared to enjoy himself. "Adventure! It's like being on a rock-and-roll tour. See all them out there. Those mobs of Docoms are my adoring fans. They've come to see, hear and feel the spectacle and power unleashed by my rock-and-roll M4. Lock and load. All kneel before me. Sacrifice yourselves unto me. All hail Michael Rollins, god of thunder and rock-and-roll."

"Docom" might have been the official Army term for unruly civilians but the grunts devised a slew of unofficial slurs to describe them. The sergeants encouraged the use of epithets with raucous affirmation. The commissioned officers encouraged their use by not protesting. Words had become weapons. Not because they were capable of injuring their victims, bullets do infinitely more damage than words, but rather their power came from their ability to enervate the soldier's sense of empathy.

Marzan never adopted the new slurs, but he did everything else he could to keep up the soldierly pretense. He often joked with the brotherhood about "smoking those Docoms" but it always came out hollow and made him feel even more like a fraud. He didn't feel connected to his unit much at all anymore. The razor was cutting him deeply.

Marzan's unit spent Christmas Eve at a Marriot. They just pulled up to the front door in their Humvees and marched right in, battle gear and all, took over a floor, cleaned out the bar, and proceeded to ransack the place. Who was the manager going to call? The police? What, and risk getting his business labeled as hating the troops? No way. He just smiled and cleaned up the mess.

The next morning, the manager found a note stroked by a sergeant telling him who to call about getting a reimbursement. The Army's notion was that money could paper over any sin. That's how they operated back in Shariastan. Bulldoze a house, kill a family goat, mistakenly drop a cluster bomb on a wedding reception. "So sorry about that. Here... here's a stack of hundreds that'll make everything right."

Five days after Christmas, Marzan's unit drove west from St. Louis on I70. Rumor was they were headed to Denver and that there was going to be some real action. Colorado's governor had just resigned under pressure from D.C. His replacement was much more in tune with the D.C. program. Having a much more flexible interpretation of Posse Comitatus—the 1878 Act barring the Army from being used as domestic police—the new governor called in the DSF to restore order.

The National Security Agencies' internet spies uncovered a fomenting, organized civil disobedience movement. The snoops, snitches, and worms trolling the net gleaned details of a major anti-DC rally that was going to erupt in January. Welfare proles burning cars and smashing windows in the name of hunger was a somewhat acceptable expression of frustration to the feds, but openly challenging Washington's authority was not to be tolerated—anywhere. In other words, gathering to cry out, "Help Us!" was permissable as it validated D.C. But gathering together to shout, "fuck off!" was considered sedition. Secessionist protests were considered contagious as well. If not utterly crushed by military force, they might trigger a plague of nationwide revolt. There was no way D.C. was going let that happen. No way.

"Aw, that's bullshit! They canceled the Superbowl," Rollins whined as he scanned his smart phone. "I guess we're gonna have to make our own superbowl, then. Yep, the big game's in Denver. Domestic Security Force versus The Insurgents. What's the Vegas line on that one? C'mon Jimmy, who's favored?"

97

Marzan didn't answer.

Rollins answered for him. "You pussy. I'll take DSF and lay the 56 points. It's gonna be an ass whuppin'."

Their convoy rumbled down I70, completely commandeering the left lane. Any civilian vehicle brazen enough or unwitting enough to occupy that lane was run off the road.

Marzan thought about the Indians as they drove. It took forces of the United States more than a century to conquer the vast continent, requiring decades of cavalry assaults, cheap liquor, gulags, and barbed wire to finally annihilate the resistance of the stone-aged natives. "Manifest Destiny" was what they called it. The name gave the massacre a divine purpose which erased the guilt.

The Indians just didn't have the technology or the numbers or the organization to win. But they fought like hell for a century. They fought for their property, their lives, and their unalienable rights. They fought bravely and gallantly in a long war until finally the Nez Perce, frozen, hungry, their elders killed, surrendered to the U.S. Cavalry. "Hear me, my chiefs! I am tired; my heart is sick and sad. From where the sun now stands, I will fight no more forever." The words of Chief Joseph.

America is a big and often inhospitable place. Even the Japanese Admiral Yamamoto, in perhaps the finest endorsement of the Second Amendment ever made, shied away from the prospect of invading a nation with a "rifle behind every blade of grass." But now the Domestic Security Force was poised to subdue the entire continent in less than a few months. Yamamoto and George Armstrong Custer didn't have Black Hawk helicopters, infrared, predator drones, fifty-caliber weapons, or an enemy disarmed by the Firearms and Neighborhood Security Act.

The DSF crossed the Kansas and Colorado state line, but their advance was halted in Limon by a blizzard. They sheltered in their vehicles with their Humvee engines idling through the night. The wind whistled down on them from the west. Drifts of snow piled against their wheels.

"What are you doing?" asked Marzan.

"I'm taking a piss. What does it look like?" answered Rollins as he finished up.

"What are you gonna do with that bottle?"

"Here, you want a swig?"

Marzan turned away in disgust. Rollins made his way to the back and opened the door. Ice crystals and frozen air poured in.

"What the fuck, Gollum?!" cursed Wingate. "Close the fucking door!"

Rollins tossed his specimen out the back and pulled the door shut. The temperature inside instantly dropped twenty degrees.

"Man, I didn't sign up for this blizzard shit," complained Specialist Wingate.

"It's just snow. No big deal," said Sergeant Tjaden.

"That's because you're from North Dakota, asshole. I'm from Florida. Look at it out there. You can't see nothin'. We're gonna be buried alive."

"Just relax. It'll blow over by morning."

They hunkered down for the night and the storm eventually blew over, just as Tjaden had predicted. The column followed snowplows back down the highway. The clouds disappeared by mid-morning revealing an alien world to the soldiers from the Rust Belt, and the South, and the coastal ghettos. It was treeless and desolate, a blazing white earth from horizon to horizon under a cloudless, beaming blue sky. A cold, blinding sun climbed towards its zenith. They might as well have been invading the moon with all its starkness.

Marzan thought about how the Germans must have felt gobbling up thousands of square miles of Russian nothingness in the early days of Operation Barbarosa. How they must have wondered how it could possibly be worth it to conquer so much empty space. That endeavor didn't end so well for the *krauts* when the winter came and their diesel fuel turned into jello and their toes turned black.

DSF arrived at their destination after nightfall, along with the clouds that rolled down from the north and filled up the sky and blotted out the stars and moon. They set up camp at Denver International. By morning, the snow came again and swirled and whipped about on the wind, never seeming to reach the ground. It was bitter cold.

Rumors were swirling around as well. Militias were forming. Police units were dissolving. National Guards were defecting. Government offices were over-run. The words "civil" and "war" were being connected together in a contemporary context for the first time in a hundred and fifty years.

"This is exciting shit!" Rollins declared. "Smokin' them dumbasses in the ghetto was getting kinda dull."

Jimmy Marzan spent that morning vomiting. He blamed it on altitude sickness.

Chapter 15

"Mr. Clayton, I'm going to have to ask you to stay in town," advised the portly detective from the sheriff's department. He talked with his mouth still full of processed the chicken he had just picked out of a blue eagle package. He had arrived shortly after the deputies, who never bothered to remove their shades during their perfunctory examination of Vaughn's house. A wrinkled blue suit draped the detective's slouching frame. He wore his thinning hair combed forward to mask a prematurely receding hairline. His notepad and cheap Bic pen never left his pocket.

"You don't look like a detective," Vaughn remarked. Vaughn encouraged and even pleaded with the deputies and detective to search everything and spend as much time as they needed at the crime scene. He showed them the muddy footprints in the hallway that they had missed. He showed them the tire tracks in the driveway. He even offered them Jessica's journal, but they weren't very interested in any of it.

"What gives? Am I the suspect?" Vaughn asked.

"Not technically," answered the detective. "Let's just say you're a person of interest for now. A lot of these cases end up where the wife just up and left. A lot of other times, someone she knew was responsible."

"What do you mean? I hear about kidnappings for ransom all the time. None of those were people they knew." Vaughn felt a rage percolate up into the blood vessels of his face.

"We need to rule out the obvious possibilities first."

"Well I didn't do anything to my wife. And she didn't leave. She wouldn't leave her daughter half frozen to death. She was kidnapped. Find the kidnappers. You're wasting time."

"We're not saying you did it," answered the detective, spitting out crumbs as he spoke.

"Then tell me what I can do to help find her. I'll do whatever you want. I'll take a polygraph, anything. Just find her!"

"Vaughn, let me be honest with you," said the detective as he wiped his greasy fingers on the insides of his suit pants pockets. "You know that your wife isn't the only one that's been kidnapped around here. Hell, we had fourteen kidnappings in the county this month alone. And half of them are relatives of cops, for crying out loud."

"What are you trying to say?"

"I'm trying to say that you need to chill out a little. It's going to take some time. We have to deal with these things on a first-in, first-out basis. So just relax and try not to worry so much."

"What? Try not to worry? My wife is missing! How can you tell me to not worry?!"

"Just calm down...easy." The detective put his greasy paw on Vaughn's shoulder. "Relax. The feds will be getting involved, soon. These kidnappings are becoming a national epidemic. There's been too many of these disappearances while law-enforcement resources have been devoted to higher priorities. But all that's about to change. I'm sure you've heard of TAPSRA?"

"What?"

"The president signed it back in September—The Anti-Kidnapping and Public Safety Restoration Act."

"I just want you to take some prints or something. Do your job."

"You've been watching too much TV. We don't do it that way. Just sit tight, wait for the ransom call." The detective balled up his foil wrapper, tucked it into his pants pocket, and handed Vaughn one of his cards. He walked out the door and disappeared into the cold with the deputies. Vaughn and tiny Brooke, who was watching a DVD about mermaids, were alone in the house again.

"Where's mommy?" she asked, looking up from the TV.

Vaughn mustered a smile. Looking down into her wide little eyes, he was deeply afraid that they would never see her mother again. *How will I manage?* he wondered.

He checked his voicemail for the 30th time...still nothing. He contemplated making the dreaded call to Jessica's mother but he couldn't do it just yet. He had to process things a little more.

He began to pace. *What is wrong with these people?* he asked himself. *Can't they see that she didn't just leave? All of her things are here, even her coat. Why would she tear the house apart? If she left, she wouldn't have left the door open and Brooke to freeze. She couldn't leave Brooke. No way. Do they seriously think I did something to her?*

Brooke went back to her mermaids. Vaughn let her entertain herself for the better part of the day while he sat and waited for a ransom call. He checked his phone seven times to make sure the ringer was on or that the battery was still alive or that an incoming message alert hadn't been missed.

Nothing.

At eight o'clock, he put Brooke to bed and poured himself a whiskey. He was not normally one to drink it straight, but somehow the thought of its potency appealed to him at that moment. He paced with his cell phone in one hand and his drink in the other, waiting, contemplating the enormous endeavor of cleaning up his decimated house. He downed the drink and checked the phone an eighth time.

Nothing.

He poured himself another whiskey and walked from room to room taking inventory and looking for clues. He checked the phone a ninth and tenth time. Exhausted, he migrated back into the family room and fell into his sofa.

He decided that reclamation of the household was far too big a task for nine p.m. He got up and poured another drink. He resisted the urge to look at his phone, that time. *The god damn phone,* he thought. *Why won't it ring?* He was inclined to smash it to bits. *No, that won't help.* He was helpless. There was nothing he could do. He put his face into his hand and started to weep. He composed himself and took another drink. For an instant, he worried that he would be too hung over for work the next day. Then he remembered he was unemployed. *Perhaps the timing's perfect,* he thought. *I can dedicate all my time to finding Jess.* He sucked on the sour ice cubes from his empty glass. *But who's going to take care of Brooke while I look for her? Mom? She'll do it. Call her.* He lifted the phone to his ear and was about to press the quick dial key but stopped himself.

By eleven p.m., the pellet stove that heated the living room was burning down, casting off its dying orange sparks. He freshened his drink again and sipped it in the darkness while the house cooled.

Call Jess's mother at least, he thought. *No, call her tomorrow when you're sober*

He dragged himself up off the sofa again and clumsily reloaded a forty-pound bag of pellets into the stove, spilling more than a handful in the process. He stumbled back towards the sofa, grabbed the whiskey bottle and cell phone and lumbered into the master bedroom. He lost his balance trying to navigate the clutter in the darkness. He fell over the overturned mattress and landed on the box spring. He lay there with his half-empty bottle and his silent cell phone for an hour, watching the red minutes click over on the digital clock on his nightstand. At 12:00, he rolled over and fell asleep.

He dreamed he was digging. He was sweeping away black dirt with his hands, trying to uncover Jessica's buried face. She was somewhere down in that dirt, suffocating. He found her hand. He dug faster, handful after handful, as fast as he could. The walls of soil collapsed back in covering her up just as he got close. A bright light flashed behind him. He heard his own voice.

"Don't look back or you might just see what's gaining on you."

He dug faster. He brushed the dirt away from Jess's face. Her eyes opened but she couldn't breathe. He dug still faster but the walls caved in again. The light brightened from behind. He looked over his shoulder again and saw the German shepherd that had terrorized him in his youth. The walls of the hole collapsed in. He clawed at the dirt in desperation but she was gone. Now he was trapped, buried by the black, sandy dirt. He heard little Brooke scream. More and more earth fell down on him in an avalanche, paralyzing him ...

"Beep. Beep."

The phone was ringing. He tried to wake up. He fumbled around for the receiver in the dark but dropped it. "Damn it!" he shouted.

"Beep. Beep."

He blindly felt around for it. "Where the hell is it?"

"Beep. Beep."

He dropped the bottle and the remaining whiskey spilled out onto the box spring. He couldn't find the phone.

"Beep. Beep."

"Where is it?!" he shouted.

"Beep. Beep."

He cursed.

"Beep. Beep."

"At last! But he couldn't get the flip top to open."

"Beep. Beep."

"Come on!" Open. Success. He put the receiver to his ear. Nothing.

"No! No!" he shouted, thinking that he had missed the call after all that. He looked into the receiver. The timer was still counting. He put it back to his ear.

"Vaughn Clayton?"

"Who is this?" Vaughn answered. No response. "Who is this?" he shouted again. He glanced over at the clock. It was 3:01. His head was spinning in a metal-on-metal screeching headache. His mouth was covered in film. "Who is this?"

"Vaughn..."

"Yes?"

"We have your wife, Vaughn."

Vaughn froze. His eyes stared at a fixed point in the darkness.
"Who are you?" he asked.

"Do you want your wife back?"

"Yes. Yes, of course. Who are you?"

"You have something we want, Vaughn."

"What is it?"

"We think you know what we want."

"I have no idea what you want!" Vaughn answered. "Money? I can't get it out bec..."

"We don't want your worthless dollars, Vaughn."

"What then?" His mind raced through his possessions. *Television, computer, furniture, car, clothing...it's all worthless junk. They wouldn't want any of that stuff,* he thought. "What do you want?" he asked.

"We want your gold, Vaughn."

"What gold?"

"You know what we're talking about. We want your gold. All of it."

"I don't have any gold."

"We know you do, Vaughn. We want those Krugerrands."

"What the hell is a Krugerrand?" Vaughn asked.

"Don't play dumb with us, Vaughn. This is your wife we're talking about. If you want to see her again, you need to deliver the Krugerrands to us."

"I don't have any Krugerrands. Please. I can get you cash but it will take a couple days."

"Like I said, we don't want your worthless dollars, Vaughn. We want your gold. We know you have a nice little collection hidden in there. Fifty ounces. We want them all. You've got two hours. Do you know where the old Mercantile Building is in Buffalo Creek?"

"The old general store? Yes, I know it."

"You've got two hours to get there. Bring your little coin collection and don't bother calling the sheriff. We'll know if you do."

"That's twenty miles from here and there's a foot of snow outside. I don't have enough gas."

"Not our problem, Vaughn. Be there. Two hours. Goodbye."
Click.

Vaughn lay motionless clutching the phone to his ear, staring into the dark. He thought that maybe he had wet the bed but then realized the spilled whiskey had run down and soaked into his khakis. He fumbled around for the lamp on the nightstand. A burst of photons nearly vaporized his eyeballs as he switched on the light. He lay back down and shielded his eyes with the inside of his elbow.

"Get up!" he slurred to himself as he swung his arm off his face, allowing the light to sear tracers into his vision.

He scrambled downstairs to the garage looking for gas. There was no way he could make it to Buffalo Creek on fumes. If he ran out, he would have to walk several miles down lonely country roads at night in the midst of a blizzard. Dying of exposure was a very real possibility.

Brooke! he thought. *Should I bring her? Absolutely not. But I can't leave her. What then?*

He found the lawnmower gas can. It had about a gallon and a half left. He went outside to the truck and carefully poured the contents in. It would be enough to get there. It was the best he could do.

He went back inside to check on Brooke. She was still asleep, tiny hands clutching her monkey. He watched her for a minute, then snuck out. He couldn't bring her, too dangerous. He picked up the phone and called his mother. It was 3:15 a.m.. He got her voicemail.

"Mom! It's me. I'm sorry to call you like this but something has happened. I need to go somewhere to help Jessica. It's an emergency. I can't take Brooke with me but I can't wait for someone to come watch her, either. I need a big, big favor. I need for you to come to my house when you get this message. I know I'm asking a lot. Brooke's asleep now and she rarely wakes up so things should be all right until you get here. I know this all sounds crazy. I'll explain everything as soon as I get back. The snow isn't coming down like it was before so you should be okay. All right? Call me as soon as you get this. If I don't answer it's because I'm in the canyons. I'll call you back as soon as I can. Okay. Goodbye."

Vaughn went back up to the master bedroom and looked over the disaster. He went to the bed and felt underneath for the shotgun. It was still there.

"Idiots!" he declared, wondering how the kidnappers missed it.

He pulled the key out from the nightstand and unfastened the cable lock.

After putting on his winter gear, he checked in on Brooke one last time. She was still asleep, snoring her tiny, whistling snores through alternating drags on her pacifier. He hoped he would make it back before she woke. He took one last look at the upheaval that was his house before quietly closing the door and getting in his truck. His mom was going to shriek when she saw it.

The snowflakes were large and falling slowly. The storm was dying. The crystalline reflections in the truck's headlamps hypnotized him as he drove. The road was packed over and slick. The county snowplows didn't run anymore, because the county was bankrupt. The volunteers would not be out for another hour or two. Vaughn prayed his mom would make it up to his house. Even if she did, she wouldn't be up for another couple of hours at the earliest. Maybe he could get back home before then.

US 285 is a treacherous span of rollercoaster highway. It climbs and dives and bends through the foothills, bluntly engineered into the steep hillsides. Since the suspension of the bulk of the State's Department of Transportation services, the road became littered with boulders that had broken loose and tumbled down the steep mountain faces along the southbound shoulder. A driver had to be wary of them as they came up fast. Now they were hidden under snow making the drive even more dangerous. Civilian Samaritans were good about pushing them to the side but that was in good weather during the daylight, and only during times when the police weren't citing them for public safety violations. There were no Samaritans out on the highway this time of night.

Vaughn turned south at Pine Junction and drove another seven miles through the town of Pine Grove which was not more than a cluster of eclectic houses and a boarded up biker bar on the banks of the winding South Platte River.

What am I going to do when I get there? he asked himself as he passed through the nearly abandoned town. He gazed down at his shotgun. He moved it down onto the floorboards with its barrel pointed away. *What will happen if the kidnappers see it?*

He thought about little Brooke, alone in the house. A terrifying sensation that she was awake and screaming in her crib came over him. No one would come for her, at least not for another couple hours.

His mind drifted to the gold coins. *What made the kidnappers think I have these things?* He recalled Mr. Croukamp at the grocery store, the night of the market crash. "Krugerrands!" he shouted in realization. *He must have them. Maybe they think I'm Croukamp! I can explain that to them. No, they won't buy it. It wouldn't be right, anyway. I can't sell him out like that. Maybe I could give Croukamp a warning before they come for him. No. It won't work. How will I handle things when I finally get there? Be honest? No. That'll get you nowhere with them. You have to lie and buy some time.*

He drove another two miles. A lonely acetylene lamp appeared in the dark, hanging over a relic payphone. The glow illuminated "1892" on the granite stone wall of the old Mercantile Building. *I made it.* He parked alongside the building by a vintage gas pump. He turned the engine off to conserve what was left of his precious fuel. The snow floated down through the golden arc of the lamplight.

Headlights appeared.

It was another truck, roaring up the highway from the south, cutting across the adjacent church parking lot. It slid to a stop with its high beams pointed directly into Vaughn's eyes, momentarily blinding him. Vaughn didn't move. He thought about the shotgun on the floor. His cell phone beeped.

"Yes," Vaughn answered.

"Step out of the truck."

Vaughn left the shotgun on the floorboard and stepped out. He put one hand up with the other clutching the cell phone at his ear.

"Where is it?"

"We need to talk," Vaughn replied.

"Where are the Krugerrands?"

"They're close."

"Show me the coins."

"Let me see Jessica first. How do I know she's okay?"

"Don't fuck with us, Vaughn. We're professionals."

"I'm not fucking with you. Please. Just show me she's okay."

"Where's the gold, Vaughn?"

"Please. Please!" Vaughn pleaded. "I'll get you what you want. Just don't hurt her. I'll get you whatever you want."

"You didn't bring it, did you?"

"Please! I'll give you everything I have. I won't tell anyone. No police. Just don't hurt her. Please. Just—"

The truck shifted into reverse and started to back up.

"No! Don't go!"

The truck's engine roared as it turned around in a spinout and tore back out onto the highway headed south.

"Please come back!" Vaughn shouted into his phone. "Don't leave!"

The call disconnected.

Vaughn ran back to the truck and turned the key but the engine would not start. It was out of gas.

Chapter 16

Crowds began assembling on a field of ice at around eleven a.m. They arrived in carpools and busses and spilled out into the snow and cold. They started fires in trashcans but the police came around on horseback and ordered them put out. This angered the freezing crowd but they complied with the pointless orders. They had been issued quite a few pointless orders by people in uniforms as of late, and they learned that exhibiting even the slightest contempt for authority encouraged brutal retaliation. The crowd of protestors chilled in their huddled masses for hours.

By two o'clock, all of the factions were represented. The Marxists, wearing their Che Guevera shirts and waving their red and black flags, had come. Their faces were obscured by red bandanas. Then their counterparts, the libertarians, with their tricorn hats, barking through their megaphones. These were deemed to be causing a disturbance and were snatched up by the police as well. The two diametrically opposed ideologies merged together in opposition to their common enemy. They shared a fleeting, fragile brotherhood of resistance which was the only warmth they would experience on that tragic day.

Other factions appeared as well: the old and the young, the conservatives and the greens (but no neocons or progressives), the potheads, the veterans, and the unemployed dads with their unshaven faces and pot bellies. Many middle-aged white men filled the park but there were also many college kids and single mothers. Blacks and Latinos and Asians had had enough as well.

There were fundamentalist and not-so-fundamentalist Christians, Orthodox Jews, Buddhists and Muslims too. They had all amassed in Denver's Civic Center Park in front of the State Capitol building with her gold leaf peeling and flaking and blowing away from her regal, romanesque dome like brittle autumn leaves in the wind. The government that had promised them so much had delivered them so little. They were tired of the empty promises. They were beginning to realize that dealing with the government had become like dealing with the devil. They were cold and exhausted, and were warmed only by their anger. They didn't know what was going to happen, but it didn't matter because their futures ceased to have relevance. They lived for the day, day by day. They had to do something. They had to take a stand. Enough was enough.

They weren't going to accept any more of the ever-expanding list of ever-increasingly vague regulations and laws. There were so many laws against selling this or buying that or going here or going there that one could be arrested for anything. They were done with the ration debit cards that bought nothing. They were tired of the obnoxious treatment by officials, the invasive, random searches, and the checkpoints—"freedom gates" as they were officially called. They would not accept any more neighborhood snitch programs designed to ferret out the "evil hoarders" who stockpiled canned food and the "energy wasters" who left their lights on too late at night. They would not tolerate waiting in thirty minute lines for toilet paper and egg noodles. They refused to accept any more *disappearing* of their neighbors.

No more were they going to tolerate beltway bureaucrats shutting off local electricity after towns exceeded their congressionally allotted energy ration because a cold front had moved in and everyone was forced to turn on their heat. No more! They were fed up with the scheduled brownouts and the gas prices doubling every four weeks and talk of reinstituting a draft and a Civilian Security Force and a Rebuild Americorps and talk of their kids soon to be kidnapped and conscripted by the Homeland Youth Brigade.

They were furious about how their pensions were confiscated under the Ghilarducci Act, which promised to save everyone's future by creating so-called "guaranteed rates of return." Their life savings—unless you worked for the government or the public employee unions—were confiscated, and the trillions of dollars were used to bail out D.C., propping up the establishment for a little while longer. Soon the guaranteed rate of return touted by the Ivy Leaguers was completely gone, wiped out in a *poof* of 200% annual inflation.

The smart ones who had bought hard assets didn't escape either. Even though they had the prudence and foresight to stash their savings in something real, Congress pillaged them as well with the Anti Greed Act (AGA) and a Windfall Profits Tax of 100% on the sale of selected commodities. "Everyone has to do their fair share," the politicians announced. In other words, "There is no escape. Your foresight and prepping and resistance is futile."

The protestors were protesting the lies more than anything. The unemployment rate officially peaked at 19%, but everyone knew that was a lie, too. It was all propaganda, not any different from what the

110

Soviets used to spout. Lies, lies, and more lies.

They saw the beltway cronies getting away with all the loot and that enraged them.

"Kill the bankers!" some howled. "Hang the Wall Street thieves!"

The Banksters had gamed the system by simply printing up a shitload of money and buying themselves a so called democracy. Under the cover of "too big to fail" and "in the interest of financial stability" they enriched themselves by the calamity. They put a gun to their own heads and shouted, "Bail us out or we'll shoot!" Big media convinced everyone that Americans had to save the bankers in order to save America as the fortunes of Main Street were tied to those of their banker overlords. It was feudalism reinvented—neofeudalism. The more desperate the situation, the more ruthless the corporatocracy became at saving themselves.

It was the same old story, told throughout antiquity. It was the twilight of Rome, the lingering death of Spanish colonialism. It was the Weimar Republic, the erosion of the British Empire, and the Jacobins had now been unleashed. Nothing ever changes.

The banks, of course, took the money and blew it on Ponzi schemes and real estate boondoggles and bets, innocuously called swaps, and collateralized debt obligations and other rackets of hedge fund plays and a mountain of increasingly worthless government debt. And before the dollar dissolved into paper unworthy of wiping oneself with, the bankers cashed it all out for Saudi oil contracts and gold bars and Swiss francs. The rats jumped the sinking ship, leaving the Main Street chumps in steerage to rearrange the deck chairs. The populist anger was building into one ferocious gale. "Kill the politicians! Kill them all!"

The initial rage of the welfare proles had finally infected the working and middle classes. Once independent and self-sufficient, now their lives too were regimented, surveilled, and increasingly dependent upon Big Brother's beneficence. They were being squeezed for protection money by local government Mafioso masquerading as code enforcers. They were terrorized by roaming thugs. And they were ignored by the police who spent their time trying to devise schemes to extract every last droplet of wealth from the dwindling earners in their jurisdictions. The latest racket was newly-devised: door-to-door tax collection they called "economic inspections." They also ramped up efforts at taxation by citation, citing people enormous fines for the most inconsequential infractions.

111

The government at first tried to deflect the furor by pointing the finger at the *evil* price-gougers. But the government soon learned that whenever they instituted price controls, the store shelves would be instantaneously swept bare of the newly bargain-priced goods. Shuttered stores paid no taxes, so the government stopped demonizing the shopkeepers. Then they tried to blame the *sneaky* Asians, but after several months, the Great Asian Liquidation—as it came to be known—was a fading memory, long removed from the crisis that continued to deepen every day.

So the government redirected their efforts toward perception management. They took control of the television, arguing that the government owned the airwaves giving them the right to commandeer them. They put on their propaganda mouthpieces to tell the people that everything was going to be okay and was, in fact, getting better. Just one more round of ten-trillion-dollar stimulus and bailouts and everything would be fixed. They censored the internet in the interests of national security and fighting terror, and they implemented martial law to make the streets safe for freedom. Safety and security became magical words capable of silencing any public dissenter.

Perhaps a lower life form, lower than even the loathsome civil servant, was that servile, submissive citizen that would always pontificate, "If you people would just cooperate with the government and give them a chance, they'll fix everything." None of those cattle-car-ready citizens were in attendance at the big nullification rally in Denver's Civic Center Park that day. The crowd grew and aside from the angry venting of "kill the bastards," it was a peaceful affair. Some fifty thousand people had braved the snow and cold by four p.m. The media, however, did not come to cover it. Not even the local news crews showed up. It was joked that their conspicuous absence was a function of it being a busy news day. There must have been a great deal of "upswings in consumer confidence" and "rising manufacturing sentiments" stories to distract them from the protest rally. Such positive stories were apparently much more newsworthy than a spontaneous gathering of fifty thousand people.

The absent media's place was taken up by the Domestic Security Force. They came in on Twentieth Street, exiting off Interstate 25. They paused briefly before the viaduct that spanned the steamy, sewage-warmed South Platte River. A gateway of two great, decorative bronze cauldrons marked the passageway into downtown. As the convoy awaited the final order to enter the city, Rollins lugged a gas can up onto the concrete base of one of the cauldrons. He poured diesel fuel into it and set it ablaze. Civilians stood and watched in silent amazement as a mechanized army crossed the shallow Rubicon and rolled into the heart of the Queen City of the Plains. The column turned south onto Broadway then east onto Colfax Avenue. They formed a line between the thoroughfares of Bannock and Lincoln Street, just behind the capitol building and her peeling gold dome.

Rollins and Marzan were in the same Humvee, again. Rollins drove this time and Marzan rode shotgun, looking green and trying not to vomit.

"What is wrong with you, dude?" Rollins asked as Jimmy opened the window and threw up down the side of the Humvee's newly urbanized gray camouflage. "Why don't you go see the doctor or something?"

"Just shut up and drive," Marzan groaned, spitting out the last of it.

Denver's mounted police took up a position south of the park along 14th Avenue. The Army-Police coalition's plan was to drive a wedge through the crowd down Broadway and then converge like a vice on the two masses, arresting the rioters by the hundreds as they squeezed out the eastern and western ends. Once arrested, they would be handcuffed with plastic binders and driven like sheep over to the convention center for processing. From there, they would be packed into 53-foot semi-trailers where they would be hauled off for indefinite detention under authority of the latest round of anti-terror legislation.

"They've gotta know what's about to go down," Rollins remarked.

The crowd watched as the forces fell into formation around them. But they weren't going anywhere. By six p.m., the roads into downtown were blocked off by barricades and reserve tanks. Big media may not have been there to capture the events, but videos were flying out to the world via cell phones. The world was tuning in and things were getting out of hand for the state's top bureaucrats who yearned for DC validation.

The wind died and the skies clouded over as night fell. The air warmed a little. At ten p.m., the Humvee loudspeakers began barking orders at the crowd. Some in the throng mocked them with one-finger salutes, but other than that, the crowd was non-combative. Rollins watched as they passed candles around. Women stood on the ice holding their feeble candles. Men with grim faces locked their arms together. The black horses huffed and snorted and shuffled around on their hooves. The soldiers, many still dressed in their tawny desert camouflage, clashing with the gray hues of their freshly painted war machines, awaited their orders.

At 11:59 p.m., the interim governor—a party apparatchik and D.C. wannabe who was watching the entire event on closed-circuit surveillance—called the president and asked what should be done. Thirty seconds later he hung up and issued the order. Thirty seconds after that, the coalition launched the tear gas canisters.

The crowd did not budge.

The sound-blasters fired their ear-piercing wails

But the crowd just locked their arms tighter and covered their ears.

The Governor called his DC master again. He hung up. He issued the next command. "Disperse them."

The Humvees roared to life. The gunners aimed their .50 calibers. The horsemen began their advance. The unarmed crowd bowed and bent, and the chains of locked arms started to break apart in places, but very few fled.

Rollins drove his Humvee up onto the grass. Just ahead of him, in the beams of his headlamps, stood a solitary figure, an unarmed man, a man who was probably someone's father and brother and son. He hurled no insults at Rollins; he simply stood there, facing the rumbling, armored war machine with the .50 caliber machine gun on its turret. His arms were at his sides.

Michael Rollins had seen him many times before back in Shariastan. He sensed his fear. Rollins-the-Brave took his hands off the steering wheel. He screwed his Osiris eye ring down onto his middle finger and glared at the unarmed man from behind his bullet proof windshield. Rollins switched on the interior light so that the resister could see him. The two men locked eyes.

Rollins did not see a human being. He only saw a sub-human savage disrespecting him, an animal refusing to obey commands, a thing secretly plotting against him. Deep down, deep within his id, beyond language, beyond consciousness, Rollins perceived a man who was several orders of magnitude more courageous than he could ever possibly be.

Anger boiled up inside of Michael Rollins. He hated that thing now, and he was going to teach that thing some respect. He grabbed the steering wheel with both hands and revved the engine. The resister didn't move. Rollins blared the air horn. The man stood fast.

Rollins had seen enough. He jammed on the gas and ran the man down with such acceleration that the Humvee bounced into the air as its wheels skidded over him. He let out an orgasmic scream as the Humvee slid to a stop in the grass. "I am Michael Rollins, god of thunder and rock and roll!"

Jimmy Marzan heaved violently but nothing but air came out.

"Did you see that?!" Rollins shouted.

"Let me out of here," Marzan shouted back.

"Did you see that, Jimmy? Holy shit. Did you see that?"

"Let me out of here!"

"Dude. C'mon man..."

In a rapid, crisp movement, Marzan took out his pistol and stuck the barrel into Rollin's temple.

"Okay. Okay. Chill out, dude," Rollins begged. "Go check him out. Maybe he'll be okay."

Marzan leaned in real close to Rollins so that the end of the barrel of his pistol touched them both. He pressed his mouth into Rollin's ear and whispered. "If I ever see you again, Rollins, I will kill you. Do you understand?"

"What the hell is wrong with you, man?"

"You listen very closely," Marzan continued, pressing the barrel deeper into Rollins' temple. "You and I—we are going to hell when we die. But if I ever see you alive again on this earth, I will send you there myself."

Jimmy Marzan leaped out of the Humvee and disappeared into the screaming darkness.

Chapter 17

After waiting about an hour at the Mercantile building, Vaughn hid his shotgun, locked up his truck, grabbed his empty gas can, and began a slow jog through the snow, south toward the village of Buffalo Creek. The snow had stopped again. A lavender glow illuminated the cloudy horizon to the east. Vaughn marched, his feet crunching through the drifts with each straining step. It was around zero degrees, judging by the way the air froze in his sinuses with each inhalation. Vaughn's toes soon lost feeling. He made it into the village just before his knees gave out. It was silent and dark. He searched around for a house with a light on or some other feature that might invite him to approach but everything was still.

Headlights appeared on the highway, coming down the hill towards him from the south. It was a sheriff deputy's SUV. Vaughn was in violation of curfew but he was too cold and too tired to hide or flee. Where would he run to anyway? The woods? He wouldn't make it very far. He stopped on the roadside and waited to surrender. The deputies' flashers came on. The SUV slowed. The driver's side window opened.

"What are you doing out here?" asked the deputy.

Vaughn wasn't quite sure how to answer. He didn't want to jeopardize Jess's life.

"I ran out of gas back up the road."

"Yeah, I thought so judging by that gas can you're holding," the deputy answered as he shifted into park. "What I meant was what are you doing out at this hour? I'm sure you're aware there's a dusk-till-dawn curfew."

Vaughn's brain raced around searching for a plausible excuse. "Uh...my wife forgot her medicine." He could tell that the deputy knew he was lying.

"Do you mind setting that can down and taking your hand out of your pocket for me?"

"No, not at all," Vaughn replied.

"I do appreciate it. I have to be careful with the way things have been, lately. You understand?"

"No problem," Vaughn answered.

"Are you armed?"

"No sir."

"Do you mind turning around for me, slowly?"

"No sir." Vaughn complied with the request.

"Can you stand right there for a second?" The deputy got out of his truck, walked up to Vaughn and frisked him from his wrists down to his frozen ankles.

"Are you arresting me?" Vaughn asked.

"I'm just being careful."

"I get that. But are you arresting me?"

"Stay right here for a second. You can put your arms down." The deputy got back into his SUV. Vaughn watched s he muttered something into his radio. The deputy paused to listen for a moment, then he turned back to Vaughn. "Get in," he ordered, as he unlocked the passenger door. "You can bring your can."

Vaughn walked around the front of the SUV and climbed in. The interior of the cab was loaded with two shotguns, an Armalite rifle, a heads-up display, and tactical gear, including a gas mask and night vision. The dashboard flickered with a fruit cocktail of blinking indicator lights. It was warm and dry in the cab, which made it nirvana for Vaughn who was certain that frostbite was getting at his toes. He thought about the excruciating pain he would feel as they thawed and their sensation returned.

The deputy looked Vaughn over for a moment, studying his expressions and mannerisms. This made Vaughn uncomfortable. Vaughn expected to be asked for his papers but the deputy just shifted into drive and the truck started north. They only had to drive for a couple minutes.

"Where's your car?"

"See it there? That pickup at the Mercantile."

They pulled into the lot and the deputy motioned for Vaughn to get out. He stepped out after him and took a long look at Vaughn's truck and the other set of tire tracks.

"Why don't you stand right here against the bumper," the deputy said as he circled to the back of the SUV.

Vaughn waited patiently while the deputy returned with his own gas can from the back of his truck. He offered it to Vaughn. Vaughn accepted the five gallons and took it over to his truck where he poured the contents in.

"I can't believe you're not arresting me," Vaughn remarked as he poured.

"For what?"

"For breaking curfew."

The deputy laughed. "That curfew's a federal order, so let the feds enforce it. Now, I will say that if DHS or ATF or DSF or any of those others catch you out here, you're probably going to jail for twenty-four hours."

"I'm sure you're right about that. I do appreciate the fuel."

The deputy glanced over at the tire tracks again. He asked Vaughn, "Is there something you feel you need to tell me? If so, I'm here to help. Are you in some kind of trouble?"

Vaughn continued pouring without answering or raising his eyes.

"We've been getting a lot of reports of bandits and kidnappers lately. I'm sure you've heard of that."

The last of the contents of the gas can dribbled into Vaughn's tank. He wanted to reveal everything to the deputy but he couldn't bring himself to do it. "I just need to get my wife her medicine," Vaughn explained. "But thanks again for the gas. You probably saved my life." Vaughn extended his free hand and the deputy shook it.

"Like I said, I'm here to help. Take my card. I'm Deputy Pritchard. Call that number. Now get home before you cross paths with one of those feds. You don't want any trouble with them."

Vaughn handed the deputy his empty can and put his in the back. He started it up. "Thanks again," he shouted out the window as he backed up and turned onto the northbound lane. He watched the deputy fade into darkness in his rearview mirror as he drove north.

Vaughn's drive was agonizing. He battled the relentless, dueling anguish for both Brooke's and Jessica's well-being. It was a drive made ever the more treacherous by the slippery, packed snow and his high speed. He reassured himself that Brooke would be fine even though he might find her in a fit of screaming. There was no way to know about Jessica, however.

Why didn't my mother call? he wondered. *Should I call the detective as soon as I get home? Should I call and tell him what happened?* Nothing could be done about any of it until he got home. There wasn't even cell reception as far out as he was. The drive would take him over an hour.

On the way home, the sun rose and the clouds dissolved. Vaughn passed a convoy of semi-trailers and army trucks on U.S. 285. They were painted khaki and were hauling storage pods and tanks sheathed in tan canvas with their guns sticking out. A column of Humvees and MRAPS followed behind. It was headed towards

119

Denver. Vaughn surmised they were shunning the more visible I25 corridor which was the more direct route from Fort Carson.

Vaughn was disheartened to find that his mother's car was not in the driveway as he pulled in. He scrambled into the house and, thankfully, found everything in the exact same state of disarray that he had left it. All was quiet. *Brooke?* He ran down the hallway to her room and eased open the door. She was still asleep. *Thank god,* he thought.

He returned to his despair over Jess. He had to decide what to do and how to set himself about doing it. He got Brooke up and fed her a breakfast of boiled egg noodles and powdered milk, which was nearly all that was left in the house to eat. He pondered opening one of his cans from his fruit cocktail hoard but that seemed extravagant.

There weren't many options for Vaughn, and the ones he did have were not good. He thought about them as he watched Brooke dance after breakfast. She moved in clumsy circles with her tiny raised hands singing, "Ring Around-the-Rosie...we all fall down," and her flexible little body collapsed in slow motion into a ball on the floor. Vaughn watched her as she performed the routine a dozen times. It amused him to think that both of them were entranced by a children's rhyme about Bubonic Plague. He mustered a smile for her on each repetition, trying to ratchet himself back from the brink. He decided there was only one option.

"When's mommy coming home?" Brooke asked.

"Soon, Princess," he answered, hoping it was true.

Vaughn waited for the call from the kidnappers but it didn't come. At nine a.m., he took out the two business cards he had been carrying. He stared at the pristine card for deputy and smudged card for the detective assigned to Jessica's case. He put one in back in his pocket. He dialed the number on the card the detective had left him. Surprisingly, the detective answered. Vaughn explained over the phone the entire early morning episode.

"Why didn't you tell the deputy what happened?" the detective asked.

"I was afraid," Vaughn answered, honestly. "The kidnappers told me not to tell the police or something bad would happen to Jessica."

"Well, you might have blown a real opportunity to catch them," the detective answered.

"I don't care if you catch them."

"What?"

"I don't care if you catch them," Vaughn repeated. "All I want is

Jess back safe."

"What kind of attitude is that? You want these guys going free out there? What if they kidnap someone else? What if they kidnap a public official next?"

"I don't care about them. I just want Jess back." Vaughn said. "So what should I do now? Are you going to investigate the site at the Mercantile? Could there be any clues there?"

The detective sighed. "We'll send someone over to check it out. But next time, let us know right away when something like this happens."

"I thought that's what I was doing."

"You're not being completely open with us. To be honest, that doesn't reflect very well on you, Mr. Clayton."

"It's not about me. It's about my daughter's mother."

"Stay in touch."

Click.

Vaughn dialed Jessica's mother before he could talk himself out of it. Her voice turned flat with the news. He tried to assure her that it was going to be all right but it was of no use.

"What are the cops doing about it?" she asked.

Vaughn wanted to say "nothing" but that would just upset her more. Instead, he answered, "They're conducting their investigation."

"Do you think she's okay?"

"I'm sure they're taking care of her."

"What makes you sure?"

"Because she's no good to them if she's..."

Jessica's mother went silent. Vaughn listened for several agonizing moments.

"Is that Mommy?" Brooke asked, tugging on Vaughn's pant leg.

"It's Grandma."

"Vaughn?" asked Jess's mother.

"Yeah?"

"Vaughn?"

"Yeah, I'm here."

Another silence followed. Vaughn looked down at little Brooke staring up at him with her saucer-like eyes and china-doll face. She reached to be picked up.

"I've heard about those kidnappings. They're happening around out here too," Vaughn's mother-in-law said.

"I'm sure they're happening in lots of places. These are crazy times."

"Vaughn?"

"Yeah?"

"You said once that if something was to happen to your family that...well..."

Vaughn knew what she meant. He knew he'd have to take matters into his own hands. The calls to the detective were a pointless exercise. "I know," he answered.

"Vaughn?"

"Yeah?"

"What are you going to do then?"

"I don't know yet," he answered, picking Brooke up and carrying her over to the kitchen to wipe her nose. "I don't know who these people are. I don't know where they are. I don't know anything about them."

"Vaughn, please get her back."

"I'll do everything I can."

"Vaughn?"

"Yeah..."

"How far will you go to get her back?"

Vaughn was aware of the likelihood that his conversation was probably being recorded. His response was measured.

"Whatever...whatever I have to do, I'll do it."

His call-waiting feature beeped. It was his mother.

Chapter 18

Vaughn slowed his truck to a stop at the end of a long line of cars. Up ahead he could see red flashers and men in black body armor with tinted face shields and M-16s. German shepherds were sniffing at car undercarriages. Vaughn stopped and turned off his engine to save his precious gas. He had to preserve what he could as his ration card was nearly exhausted.

His little blue ration debit card with a blue eagle on the face had arrived in the mail along with instructions on how to replenish it with one's bank account for a modest transaction fee. The purpose of the ration card, implemented by yet another executive order, was to combat hoarding which was blamed for the tenfold increase in the cost of fuel. Without the card, buying gas was not legal.

Vaughn waited in the checkpoint line for an hour. Brooke grew agitated. Her diaper was soiled and she was hungry and exhausted from being immobilized in her car seat. Vaughn pondered unfastening her and letting her crawl around in the front, but who knew what kind of police response that might illicit. He didn't want to give them any cause to harass him. He reached down for his backpack and took out a box of powdered milk. He poured a tablespoon's worth into her sippy cup, topped it off with tap water from a bottle, and shook vigorously. A scum coagulated on the bottom of the cup but this was normal for the ration milk. Brooke hadn't tasted real milk in two months. She also hadn't had any fresh fruit for two weeks. Vaughn had not seen any fruit in the grocery store that once brimmed with bananas and oranges and grapes. That cornucopia had been replaced with bins of potatoes, turnips, sour baking apples and sugar beets. *What the hell can you make with a sugar beet? Can a human even eat one?* There were three bins of them in the produce section.

A soot-belching eighteen-wheeler roared past him. It was painted in the gray, geometric hues of urban camouflage and the blue eagle logo that glared down at him with its sinister, all-seeing eye. The jack-hammering racket of its engine brakes startled Brooke and she began to cry. Vaughn tried to calm her with his pathetic singing of "Muffin Man." She calmed a bit, but only out of curiosity.

A winter fog swept in and cast an eerie pall while they waited. Slowly, the men in black body armor emerged from the smoky haze, making their way towards Vaughn's truck. Vaughn was thankful he'd remembered to remove his shotgun as the storm troopers did not look like they would be very tolerant regarding illegal firearms.

Vaughn guessed that the holdup was due to someone having failed an inspection. A car ahead had been directed off the road and onto the shoulder. The driver was pulled out and handcuffed, then shoved into a gray van and spirited away into the mist.

Vaughn turned on the radio. The mainstay for the past several weeks was the news about this or that government edict and how it was going to fix this or that calamity. "We are in this together," was one common refrain. "Think safety!" was another. "Report any suspicious activity," was yet another. But this morning there were no news reports, only music. Even the talk stations played music.

Maybe they've finally run out of bullshit, Vaughn thought as the inspectors made their way to his truck. He started the engine for the tenth time and pulled forward twenty feet.

"Papers please," a trooper asked, voice muffled by his opaque face shield.

Vaughn produced his license, registration, proof of insurance, ration card, and travel permit. It was a great deal of fuss for a twenty-mile drive. US 285 might as well have been a road through the Brandenburg Gate, Berlin circa 1975.

"Where you headed?" asked the trooper, bluntly.

"My mother's house. She's watching my daughter for a few days while I look for...work."

"You know you shouldn't be on the highways today unless absolutely necessary."

"What do you mean?"

"Don't you listen to the radio?"

"There's nothing but music on."

"Don't get smart with me. There's terrorist activity. It's a triple-red-alert day. They called in the Army last night to help get things under control." The trooper looked over the inside of Vaughn's truck while another officer scanned his undercarriage with a mirror, accompanied by a sniffing German shepherd.

"I didn't hear about any of that. I'm not going to be out long. I just want to get to my mom's and drop my daughter off." Vaughn was not feeling much like kissing the trooper's ass but he was savvy enough to avoid a display of contempt-of-cop. He didn't want to send the trooper into a rage, which they were prone to do.

"Stay out of downtown. And stop wasting gas. Conservation is your patriotic duty."

Vaughn couldn't suppress his disaffection any longer. "Patriotic duty?" he asked.

"Yeah," the trooper answered. "You heard me. Your *duty*. Your duty to quit wasting resources and your duty to stay out of our way so we can do our job protecting you."

Vaughn felt the hot blood pump into the vessels in his face. He tried to remain calm.

"I don't recall ever asking for your so-called protection."

"Oh, you're one of those types, eh?"

"What's *one of those types* supposed to mean?"

The trooper turned and shouted to the other officer who was still scanning the undercarriage. "Hey O'Reilly, I got me one of *those types* over here." His opaque face shield swung back to Vaughn. "What d'you say we do a full inspection on your vehicle? Huh? How about we just pull you over to the shoulder there and impound your truck? What do you think of that? Maybe you'll get it back in month or two — what's left of it anyway."

Brooke started to cry again. Vaughn looked back at her, and caught a glimpse of her blue, saucer eyes reflecting the sinister trooper in black armor. Vaughn knew he had to swallow his pride, as much as he hated to do it. "You're absolutely right," he offered in a conciliatory tone. "That wouldn't be good. Please forgive me for not being more understanding. I know you guys are under a lot of strain nowadays. Where would we be without you guys protecting our freedom? I'm sorry. I'm just frustrated about a lot of things right now."

"Well don't ever forget it." The trooper turned to the other officer. "Everything check out?"

"Looks good down here."

"Move along. And try showing a little more respect next time."

"You bet. Absolutely. Thank you, sir."

The trooper walked around the front of the truck past Brooke's window. Brooke's wide eyes were transfixed on him as he passed. She began to squirm in her car seat.

"Hang in there, kiddo. We'll be at Grandma's soon."

"Where's Mommy?" She asked.

"She's coming home soon," Vaughn answered. But as he looked at her in the rearview mirror he noticed that she was still watching the trooper and pointing at him with her tiny index finger.

"Where's Mommy?"

Vaughn started the truck and pulled forward but Brooke's little head swiveled, locked onto the trooper. When she finally lost sight of him she burst into screams.

"Mommy! Mommy!"

"Shhh." Vaughn tried to calm her.

"Mommy! Mommy! Mommy!"

The last of the black storm troopers disappeared into the fog as Vaughn pulled away from the checkpoint. Brooke didn't stop screaming until they got to Grandma's house.

Vaughn carried little Brooke into his mother's apartment. She greeted them at the door.

"What are you going to do?" she asked as she took Brooke from his arms.

"I don't know, Ma. The kidnappers might call any time and I can't leave her alone anymore."

Vaughn's mother dabbed her right eye with a wad of toilet paper, which was the closest she ever came to crying. "What's going on down here?" Vaughn asked as they sat down.

"I don't know," his mother answered before blowing her nose. "It's really bad, Vaughn. Cell phones don't work half the time. The power goes out every day. It's hard to get any information from the TV or internet. All the cable shows and channels are switched around. They don't say anything other than talk about triple-red terrorism alerts and the Chinese and how we all need to be patient and give them time to get things under control. It all sounds like a bunch of crap to me. Are they getting things under control, Vaughn?" She dabbed her eye again and put her wad of toilet paper in her pocket. She didn't want to waste it. "I don't see anything getting better. I go to the store and there's nothing to buy. What's there is all different brands now too. Most of it is stamped with that devil hawk."

"It's an eagle, mom. You know, the national symbol."

"I don't care what kind of bird it is. It looks something that came straight from Hades, swooping down on me. It's evil."

"It's just a bird."

"I never could have imagined any of this in my lifetime. It has to be worse than the Depression. There's nothing to buy. What am I going to do with a forty-pound block of cheddar cheese, Vaughn?

What am I going to do with a fifty-pound bag of flour? And those sweet potatoes? Jesus, I can't even carry the bags out of the store. There's no butter. Eggs, maybe once a week. No soap, except for lye soap. You ever use lye soap? No diapers. What do I do for diapers for Brooke, Vaughn? They've all been taken by the hospitals. I hear it's illegal to even have diapers without a ration card. Can you believe that? It's illegal to own diapers. I don't understand it, Vaughn. Why can't the government do something about it?"

"They are, Ma. But they're just making it worse."

"My friend Liz says that there was a huge protest last night at the capitol and that the Army came in and started shooting at people. She said there's dozens of dead and hundreds with really bad burns and bullet wounds and broken bones." She took out her wad and wiped her nose again. "Her husband's a doctor. She said that these Army types showed up at the hospital in the morning and started giving everyone orders."

"Orders?"

"She told them that if they have a soldier come in or any male under forty that they are to be notified about it. She gave the nurses a special phone number and a bunch of Army cell phones. Told them if they didn't call, they'd be arrested and charged with sedition. Liz thinks a lot of the soldiers are deserting." She went to the cupboard and got Brooke some crackers. "Liz's husband says that the government workers are getting death threats, and people are setting their cars on fire and shooting into their windows at night and all sorts of terrible stuff. So many government workers are leaving town that the offices are all shutting down. Liz said that even the Governor left—flew out to DC this morning."

"What else did you hear?"

"I heard from my neighbor that there are police departments fighting with each other too. There are cops arresting cops. This department is with the federal government but that department is with the state and another backs up the county. They're all fighting with each other about who does what. The cops fight while the gangs run around and terrorize everyone. It doesn't make any sense. Nobody knows who to go to for help anymore. Everyone thinks they're in charge but no one's in charge. It's chaos and no one can defend themselves because they took everyone's guns Do you want some crackers?"

"That'd be nice, Ma. I can't stay very long. The kidnappers might call."

Vaughn watched his young daughter make her way to the guest room where there was a stash of toys and books for her frequent visits. Vaughn took the crackers from his mother, followed Brooke in, and sat on the bed. Brooke set her sippy cup and crackers down on an end table, scattering crumbs everywhere. She went to the trunk where her toys were stashed and pulled out her mini teapot.

"Do you wanna sit, Daddy?" she asked.

Vaughn scrounged around in the trunk and produced two pink plastic teacups before he took a seat on the floor. Brooke was delighted. "Are we having a tea party?" he asked her.

"We are having a tea party, Daddy," she answered with a cherubic grin of white, nubby little toddler teeth.

Vaughn held out his tiny pink teacup and Brooke poured the imaginary tea. He sipped the contents, tipping the cup back with his little finger fully extended, making the noisiest slurping noise he could. Brooke giggled. She poured some tea for herself and imitated her Daddy's silly noises. He patted her head and brushed her golden hair away from her perfectly round, china-doll face.

"No Daddy!" she objected.

Apparently it was tea time and not hair time.

"Do we have any crumpets?" Vaughn asked in a cartoonish, British accent.

"Crumpets?" Brooke asked with a bewildered furrow.

Vaughn had no idea what crumpets were, but he seemed to recall that crumpets were the appropriate snack to go with tea—tea and crumpets, they always say. He nibbled at an imaginary crumpet, then handed it to Brooke who did the same. They sipped imaginary tea and ate imaginary crumpets as the white mist swirled around outside the window.

"I have to go now, Brooke," Vaughn said, not knowing how long it would be before he would see her again.

"Bye, Daddy," she answered. The toy box having grabbed her attention.

"I have to go get your Mommy."

"Mommy's coming home?" she asked.

"Mommy's coming home," Vaughn answered.

He grasped her tiny arm and pulled her close, swallowing her up in his arms as if she were a teddy bear. He nuzzled her on the neck with his stubbly face which made her squeal and laugh. He couldn't imagine a reason to live if he were to lose her, too. A lump crawled up and lodged itself into the middle of his throat. He had to escape before it took him apart in front of his mother. She was intolerant of blubbering. Vaughn let go of Brooke, pushing her gently towards the toy box.

"I'll come down as often as I can, Mom." He made his way to the door.

"She'll be fine," she answered. "Just get Jess home."

Vaughn turned back and hugged her.

Chapter 19

The snow was falling again as Vaughn coasted into the last gas station. He didn't have enough fuel to make it home. To his dismay, he found the pumps were covered with yellow baggies indicating "out of service." His options were to leave his truck and walk the last five miles or beg the storekeeper to sell him a gallon illegally. Neither option was very appealing.

He noticed a shadowy figure making his way down the road toward the station. He was not a local; he had a vagabond appearance dressed in a frayed, black trench coat. Vaughn decided it best not to leave his truck behind.

He went up to the door of the store but found it locked. The lights were on inside so he knocked. The shopkeeper came to the door, looking irritated. Vaughn made himself look as pathetic as possible. The shopkeeper unlocked the door and let him in. The vagabond followed behind him..

"Ain't got no gas," said the keeper

"Please," Vaughn begged, "all I need is a gallon, even half a gallon—just enough to get home. I'll give you all I have." Vaughn pulled out his wallet and began counting off bills...ten...twenty...thirty.... The shop keeper just rubbed his handlebar mustache, peering through his squinty eyes while Vaughn counted.

"Even if I had any, I couldn't sell any to you today. I'm at my quota."

The vagabond who followed Vaughn into the store stepped toward them. His black stocking cap was pulled down low, almost over his eyes. He was shivering.

"Would you sell it to him if he had a black card?" the vagabond asked.

The shopkeeper's squinty eyes popped wide open.

"A black card? Let's see it, then."

The vagabond turned to Vaughn first. "If I can get you some gas will you give me a ride?"

Vaughn considered it for a moment. It sounded like a bandit's ruse but he was desperate. "Where to and how much gas will you get me?"

"Not too far. I'll tell you outside." He reached into the breast pocket of his overcoat and pulled out a money clip containing a wad of Reagans—$500 bills—and a black credit card with a luminescent gold eagle on the face. It had no other identifying marks other than the matte data strip on the backside. "Here." He handed it to the shopkeeper.

"How much do you need?" asked the shopkeeper.

"Fill it up."

"You got it. Pump number two. Just put the yellow baggie back on when you're done."

Vaughn couldn't believe his spectacular good fortune. It was too good to be true. He couldn't remember the last time he had a full tank of gas. But there had to be a devil in the details, somewhere. Vaughn and his new benefactor stepped outside to the pump.

"This isn't some sort of a scam, is it?" Vaughn asked, as he pulled the yellow baggie off the nozzle and stuck the spout into the tank. "Are you going to rob me?"

"No. But if I was, do you actually have anything I'd want?"

"So where am I taking you, then?"

Vaughn noticed that the vagabond was standing in front of Vaughn's license plate, blocking it from the view of the shopkeeper who spied on them from the inside of the shop, twisting the ends of his moustache again as he watched.

"Let's wait until we're out of here," he said as he bent down and began unscrewing the license plate.

"I really don't have anything valuable," Vaughn said. "Anything you take from me would be worth far less than this tank of gas you're giving me."

"I suppose I could steal your truck but I don't imagine I'd get very far with all the checkpoints." He tucked the license plate into his overcoat.

"Why are you taking that off?"

"Just to be safe. There's a lot of snitches around. A black card tends to draw attention. I'll put your plate back on up the road a mile or so."

"Are you in trouble or something?"

"Who isn't these days?"

The gas pump clicked off.

"Let's go. Back out over there so he can't read your back plate." He winked, dispelling some of Vaughn's anxiety. They got in and Vaughn backed out and drove down the road.

They travelled a mile in silence. Vaughn was too nervous to

come up with any small talk. It didn't matter anyway. His passenger didn't seem like a fan of idle chat. His rider stared directly ahead, almost without blinking.

At what point does he take out his gun? Vaughn wondered.

"Stop here. I've got to pick something up over there. Hang on a second. You aren't going to leave me, are you? I still have your plate. I can find you."

"No, I won't."

He got out and jogged into the woods just off the shoulder. Vaughn felt an urge to stomp on the gas and leave him, but his integrity made him wait—he did make a deal after all. His passenger retrieved a loaded trash bag hidden in the brambles and snow. He opened the passenger door and placed it in the cab on the floor. Then he walked to the front of the truck. Vaughn tried to discern what was hidden inside the bag while the vagabond screwed his license plate back on. Vaughn didn't quite have the nerve to peek into it though.

"Okay, let's go."

They continued up the canyon road toward Vaughn's house.

"This would be a great spot for an ambush," the rider observed. "See that bend up ahead? You could block it off just around the corner there with a couple of trees or wrecked cars. They wouldn't see it until it was too late. It'd take forever to back up to that turnout we just passed back there. And there's all kinds of cover for extraction. Look at that over there, see that ridge? It's perfect."

"So will you tell me who you are?" Vaughn interrupted.

The vagabond grinned. "Yes. That's a fair question." He took off his stocking cap revealing his high and tight haircut. "My name is James—James Marzan. You can call me Jimmy. But I'd appreciate it if you didn't tell that to anyone until I'm long gone." He loosened his overcoat revealing a khaki-colored t-shirt. He opened his bag and stuffed his hat into it revealing the barrel of an M4.

"You're a soldier."

"Yeah, I guess. I was anyway."

"Was?"

"Is that a problem for you?"

"No, no. Not at all."

"Look, I don't want to get you in any kind of trouble. I just need a ride a few miles down the road towards Bailey. Maybe you got some food I can eat before you take me out there? Maybe some civilian clothes would be nice, if I could borrow some. This old coat smells like piss. I had to pay a bum a Reagan for it."

"I can do that for you but I—"

"Don't worry. I'll never tell anyone you helped me. I'm not a rat. I ain't going to get captured, anyway. Not alive. They don't take deserters alive."

"You deserted?"

"Yeah, I guess. I guess I didn't really dig on shooting civilians too much. There's a whole lot of us that feel that way. Half a division running around out here, now."

"My mother said that the Army shot up a riot in Denver the other night. Is that true?"

"It was hardly a riot. But yeah, we did. Why do you think I'm here now?"

"How could they do that?"

"Soldiers follow orders. It's what we do. Hell, we did worse than shoot people."

"Like what?" asked Vaughn.

Jimmy turned and looked out the window as they flew past the snow-covered ponderosas closing in on either side of the narrow road. "This whole stretch of road is an insurgent's wet dream. You get a lot of patrols through here?"

"Like cops?"

"Like Humvees, MRAPS. Military hardware."

"I haven't noticed a whole lot of that. I guess I've seen a couple come through this way." Vaughn changed the subject. "I have some food at the house," he offered. "And you're welcome to have some of my clothes too. I really appreciate the gas."

"So you're not worried about giving aid and comfort to a *terrorist*?"

"I thought terrorists kill civilians. It sounds like tyou're the opposite."

"So what's your name?"

"Vaughn Clayton."

"What's your story, Vaughn?"

Vaughn came right out with it. "My wife's been kidnapped. I'm trying to get her back."

"What the fuck?"

Jimmy Marzan was suddenly afflicted with the realization that Vaughn's plight might be a great opportunity for him. *Funny how God always presents us with opportunity for redemption,* he thought.

"So who took her?" Jimmy asked.

"I've no idea."

134

"What's the ransom?"

"They think I have Krugerrands."

"Gold? And my guess is you don't have any."

"They got me mixed up with my neighbor, I think."

"What are you going to do, then? Rip your neighbor off? Are the police working on it?"

"They got bigger problems to deal with."

"Right."

They turned up Vaughn's road and pulled into his driveway. Marzan scanned the tree line and neighbor's windows for spooks before exiting the truck. "You've got to be wary of the 'see something, say something' types," he said. He took his stocking cap out of his bag and put it back on. He pulled it down low and he flipped up his coat collar obscuring as much of his face as possible. He grabbed his bag and the two of them hustled into Vaughn's house.

"You mind if I take my stuff out here?" Jimmy asked.

"Not at all, but it might make more sense to do it in the guest bedroom, back there."

Marzan made his way into the bedroom with Vaughn trailing behind him.

"I apologize the house is so messed up. The kidnappers ransacked the place and I haven't had time to..."

Marzan didn't appear concerned with Vaughn's housekeeping. He tossed his bundle down on the mattress and tore the double-lined trash bag apart.

Vaughn's eyes widened. "Is that an AR-15?"

"It's an M-4. AR is civilian, semi-auto." He ticked off his inventory. "I got a hundred and eighty rounds of 5.56. Gen 5 night vision. Had to let the radio go—they put GPS in them. There's a med kit with sutures, gauze, antiseptic, forceps, and a plastic thing to hold over a chest wound so the air doesn't leak out." Marzan turned to Vaughn and grinned, punctuating his gory imagery. "There's two tear gas grenades, a silencer there, gas mask, flashlight, one big motherfucking knife, a fat wad of Reagans, and a Gideon's Bible. I'm wearing my Kevlar. All this and my fatigues, this coat that smells like piss, and my black card—which they'll soon trace to that gas station back down the road. That's everything I own in this world, Vaughn. Oh yeah, and my 9mm."

"So what's your plan? Where are you going? Are you going home? Where is home?"

Marzan chuckled. "Irvine California. The Army probably

already told my family I've done something terrible. They'll have that place staked out. There's no going home for me until it's all over."

Chapter 20

Adjacent to the spired terminal at Denver International Airport stood a forty foot statue of the Egyptian god of the afterlife. The half-man–half-jackal deity, erected to herald a touring exhibit of antiquities, stood guard over the Domestic Security Force's headquarters. The DSF nick-named him "Jackie" and rechristened the DSF base as "Camp Anubis."

Rollins spent his morning disassembling, cleaning, and reassembling his rifle. He could break it all the way down to the firing pin and reassemble it blindfolded. He spent an hour after that surfing the list of armed forces approved websites. He ate brunch, then went to the lounge.

Many new faces had just arrived at camp, coming from Fort Carson located just eighty miles to the south. They came well-equipped, bringing along with them all their newest and most expensive toys including urban MRAPS, tanks, gunships, freshly painted Humvees, and predator drones. It was an awesome spectacle of modern mechanized Shock and Awe. But Rollins felt the potpourri of clashing camouflages and jumbled command structures was compiled haphazardly. It seemed rushed or sloppy. The new DSF lacked continuity. It made him anxious.

The rumor circulating among the grunts was that they were all being combined into one super, mixed division, fully mechanized and nearly self-sufficient. They were being trained to live off the land, which meant requisitioning whatever they needed from the civilian populace and paying for it with Reagans and Roosevelts.

Blisters of civil unrest flared up like teenage acne all across the western states. Idaho, Montana, Utah, Nevada, west Texas, Oklahoma, and Wyoming, in addition to Colorado, all had situations that were coming to a head. Denver was seen as something of a rebel lynchpin. It was the biggest city to dissolve into chaos and if it could not be subdued quickly, the anti-federalist rebellion might erupt nationwide. The feds were giving the DSF a force upgrade to better equip it to re-establish federal hegemony.

Further complicating matters were the massive number of AWOLs that had undermined the DSF's operational effectiveness. The division was hampered by hundreds of defections in the wake of the

Denver Civic Center security operation—or "massacre" as it was known to the civilians.

"Traitor," Rollins mumbled as he marched into the lounge. He took a seat on a sofa and kicked his boots up on an ottoman. He was thinking about Jimmy Marzan while screwing his ring down on his finger.

The lounge was a large tent containing casual furniture, a 100 inch television, a ping-pong table, a weight set requisitioned from an Aurora sporting-goods store, and a video game system where soldiers could take a break from real firefights by immersing themselves in virtual ones. Rollins fixed his eyes onto America One, a brand new cable news network that combined the top talents of Fox, CNN, NBC, CBS, ABC, and MSNBC into one super-network with one singular message. America One only provided news that was fit for public consumption and served the greater good.

"An illegal demonstration in Denver turned unexpectedly violent yesterday," said the reporter. "Widely reported acts of violence and vandalism, including several assaults and arson, left officials with no choice other than to take action. Units of local police, the Colorado National Guard, and the U.S. Army's Domestic Security Force were called in to restore order. We have received word that at least six members of the joint security cooperative sustained serious injuries. One soldier remains in critical condition at Denver General..."

Rollins was disappointed by the report. He didn't recall any National Guard anywhere near the riot that day. What he heard was that the Colorado Guard was deployed 200 miles away in Grand Junction. *Probably too risky to put weekend warriors into a battle with their neighbors*, Rollins thought. He had heard that the Guard was suffering terrible rates of attrition. Some units had lost 50% of their troops. *Just wait 'til those traitor videos find their way into the Guard's cell phones. Soon there won't be any of them left. It don't matter, anyway. They're worthless.* America One reported two dozen civilian casualties. Rollins knew it was more like a three hundred.

The entire Denver situation continued to explode. The morning after the sweep of Civic Center Park saw a flurry of sporadic violence. An enraged civilian firebombed a federal office in the suburb of Lakewood. The Denver police force was decimated as nearly two-thirds of their force stayed home from work to protect their families.

"Yo Gollum!" shouted a shirtless private named Black who had just finished pumping himself up with a set of curls.

"Why do you call me Gollum?" Rollins asked.

"Cuz of that ring you're always fucking with and cuz you look like an ugly-ass troll, too."

"Fuck you."

Black sat down next to Rollins. His tone changed. "So, did you hear?"

"Hear what?"

"Another officer went AWOL. That's three this week."

"Who?"

"Captain Rick!"

"No."

"Yep. He was out with Hazlitt this morning. Intel-gathering and such. Well they took ten guys out and I guess nine never came back. Can you believe that shit?"

"Maybe they got ambushed?"

"Nope. They sent Cheeks back in a Hummer all by himself. I guess he had second thoughts about defecting. Drones spotted the torched-out Hummers parked at an abandoned grocery store. No bodies. Old Captain Rick and his boys just melted away into the population."

"They ought to shoot those bastards."

Black nodded faintly.

"I'm telling you, they should've micro-chipped us all at basic and said, 'next asshole that even talks about deserting and we're dialing a hellfire missile right up your ass.'"

"Well, they're doing just the opposite. Word is brass is pissing their pants over all these defections. They're worried the whole division will bug out, so they're downplaying everything. I guess they don't want to give it any more legs."

"Command's got a pussification complex."

"Yeah, politics I guess."

Rollins was disappointed that Black spoke of the deserters with insufficient scorn. The rat wheel in Rollin's brain started to turn. "So tell me, Black, what do *you* think we should do with deserters?" he asked, with his lie detector glare turned on.

"Hey, chill out dude. I'm just telling you what I heard. That's all."

"Well, what are you gonna do, Black? You gonna turn traitor too? You gonna puss out on us? Become an insurgent? Go join Al Cracker?"

"Fuck you, Gollum," Black replied and stormed off.

Rollins added Black to his personal watch-list—soldiers he

intended to keep an eye on and frag if necessary.

Rollins attended a briefing that afternoon in the Big Top—the headquarters tent.

"As part of the new Block-and-Control strategy," said the new colonel brought in from the National Security Agency, "municipal water purification and private gas stations will be shut down in the city and county. Potable water and fueling stations are going to be set up at seventeen points around the city. See them here on the map? Civilians will need to go to these centers to obtain their drinking water and fuel. While there, they will need to present their ration card for scanning. This is essential intelligence gathering. We're building a database on every citizen. We're going to track the movements of everyone that stays in the city. This is...well, think Fallujah, people. These distribution centers will be manned by what's left of the civilian police units. Civilian police need a job that'll better leverage their unique talents. What we've learned is that they tend to lose discipline when the opponent is returning fire." The colonel paused and chuckled faintly. "When we describe civilian police as 'paramilitary' it has less to do with *military* and more to do with them being *paralyzed* when it comes to high intensity situations." The soldiers laughed at the colonel's joke, just like they chuckled when the colonel back in Shariastan mocked the local police. "Gentlemen," he continued, "we know that the police are poorly conditioned and insufficiently trained for counter-insurgency. They are a liability, so we need to keep them out of the way so we can conduct our operations efficiently. I'm sure they will protest, but inside they will be relieved. They aren't ready for this. Counter-insurgency is a quantum leap from writing speeding tickets."

The colonel shuffled through his notes. "Now, that being said, we don't want to alienate them. Being a part of the community, the civilian police have some sense of what is going on out there. They have ears in the field. That makes them a valuable information resource. We have to keep the communication lines open with them. Always maintain a cooperative attitude with civilian police, even if they are essentially useless."

Rollins raised his hand.

"Question?"

"Why don't they just evacuate the city?"

"Some have suggested that—that the metro area be evacuated. Unfortunately, evacuating two million people is an inconceivable logistical nightmare. How would we move two million people? Where would FEMA house them? Feed them? Not to mention the march to the relocation facilities would be portrayed as some sort of a modern day 'Trail of Tears' by the insurgents. Talk about a public relations disaster. So we are left with the prospect of an Army division of 15,000 men patrolling a city that spans over 400 square miles with double that area in wooded, mountainous terrain immediately to the west. Historically, it has taken an entire division to sweep and clear a single square mile in one day. We have to do better than that. I don't know about you all, but I don't want to be here for eighteen months. We must conduct our operations with highest efficiency."

"Cakewalk," Rollins muttered under his breath.

The Colonel continued. "We've learned from past experience that any endeavor to pacify an enormous civilian population that has access to arms, that has empty bellies, and has nothing to lose is going to present us many unique challenges. You are each expected to rise to meet those challenges."

"Gentlemen, in all of the history of warfare, there have been only three kinds of soldiers. There are conscripts who are unmotivated and require a tremendous amount of leadership. Conscripts are what we used to refer to as 'cannon fodder'. Then there are professional soldiers who are here by choice. That would be each of you. You are self-motivated to do your job — to accomplish your objectives and follow the rules of engagement. But gentlemen, there is another type of soldier. He is the insurgent...the guerrilla. The guerrilla doesn't care about you, the Geneva Convention, treaties, your bullshit rules of engagement, or even rotating back home in one piece. The guerrilla is already in his home. He fights you from within it. His only mission, his only reason for existence is to drive you out or to kill you. He has nothing to lose. Dying might even be considered a luxury to him."

"The guerrilla is not an American. He is not a patriot. He is a rebel. He is an anarchist. He'd murder your grandmother if he thought it would damage your morale. Do not forget that when you encounter him." The Colonel handed the podium over to a captain who briefed them on the details of the block-and-control strategy.

Wars with an enemy who has a "fuck it" mentality should be avoided at all costs — at least according to Sun Tzu. But every generation of insular, BMW-driving officer candidate comes to believe: "This time it is different. This time, my side has total technological and tactical superiority. This time, I cannot lose." But from the third century Huns to the Warsaw Jews to the Viet Cong to the Mujahideen, the lesson is retaught to the patricians who make up the officer class. Some officers are so dense that they have to be retaught respect for insurgents three times on three different continents.

Nothing ever changes.

The captain described an expansive network of insurgent cells that were feared to be metastasizing in the wake of the Civic Center Park massacre. The concern was that a little dose of leadership from the defecting Army and Guard officers might be just enough to galvanize those guerrillas into a pesky adversary, especially under the cover of the wooded foothills to the west.

An occupation force may have tactical superiority, but the resister still has many advantages. His simple strategy is to poison the mind of the occupier, to make him constantly fear that he could be killed by a sniper or a bomb at any moment wherever he goes. The guerrilla strives to take away every sanctuary, to make the occupier hold his rifle in one hand while he wipes his ass with the other, to break down his morale and ultimately his mind with paranoia.

"Thank god it's winter," a soldier near Rollins smirked. "I bet they're loving the cold."

The plan was to force the populace to submit by keeping them dependent and properly supervised with daily check-ins for water, fuel and rations. Any uprising of middle-aged men would be snuffed out by DSF patrols or would quickly dissolve due to hunger and cold. Hegemony would be quickly restored.

If that failed, there was a Plan B—aka the Sherman Doctrine. But that was only if Denver could not be subdued and the insurrection was beginning to fuel a regional revolt.

When Rollins heard the rumor of Plan B, he almost got an erection. But somewhere—somewhere buried deep down within his simian brain—a synapse flickered. Rollins briefly understood why the officers, who had heard of Plan B already were defecting. He shook the subversive thought out of his mind with a vigorous nod and resumed anxiously twisting down his precious Osiris eye ring.

Chapter 21

Vaughn spent three days waiting for the kidnappers to call. He barely ate or slept. He waited on his sofa, checking his phone for missed calls every ten minutes. Half the time his phone's display read "no service."

While Vaughn brooded, his new roommate paced through the house and peered out the windows at the occasional cars that roared up the road.

"Don't worry. That's just the mailman."

"Oh, I'm not worried," Jimmy answered.

"Why are you always going to the window every time a car comes by then?"

"Just curious who it is. If they knew I was here and they were coming, we wouldn't hear anything at all." But Jimmy still went to the window every time he heard a car.

The kidnappers did not call. With each passing hour, Vaughn's face became more ashen. His body melted deeper into his sofa. He did not yield to his temptation to call the detective assigned to his case. He had little faith in the police. *Besides, if they had new information, they'd let me know*, he thought. *Jimmy's probably relieved I don't call them anyway.*

"You hear that?" Jimmy called.

"I don't hear anything," Vaughn mumbled.

"Listen..."

Vaughn listened.

"It's a buzzing. Real faint. Hear it?"

"No."

"You know what that is?"

"I've no idea. I don't hear anything."

"Shhh. It's a drone. You can't hear it unless the wind blows just right. There...listen..."

"I don't hear anything," Vaughn bristled, finally succumbing to his temptation and dialing the detective. The voice on the other end sounded disinterested, as if it had more important things to do. Vaughn hung up. He knew that would happen.

"No answer?" Jimmy asked.

"They're busy. They're probably on a more high profile case. Got to secure those brownie points with the feds, I guess."

143

"Maybe," Jimmy said. "Or maybe they're busy trying to get their families out or something."

Whatever the excuse, it ruined what little confidence Vaughn had that his detective was making progress. There was almost no law enforcement anymore, unless it was martial law enforcement which meant the manning of checkpoints and curfew patrols by police with frayed nerves and itchy trigger fingers. Vaughn returned to his brooding.

Marzan escaped Vaughn's tension by checking his email accounts and forum posts. Almost everything was encoded.

"Lucifer Rising, 1201."

"In through the out door."

"Papa say, 'The bell tolls for thee.' Lock and load."

"Elvis has left the building."

There were hundreds of similar, seemingly meaningless, disconnected emails and tweets sent from encrypted IP addresses. They might be specific orders or coordinates or maybe coded events with dates and times. Marzan had only a vague idea of what they meant, but something was in the works. It was comforting to see it. It meant that, in the least, an insurgent disinformation campaign was underway.

Marzan had seen it before from the occupier's perspective. The most effective way for a guerrilla force to cloak its operations is by filling the airwaves and the internet and the mail and the phone lines and the ear drums with a tsunami of phony assassination lists and fake military targets and phantom weapons caches and vague gibberish and every conceivable lie on top of lie. Its purpose was to confuse and to spook the occupier and to create cover for the underground's real communications. The occupier's intelligentsia couldn't possibly sift through it all and get to the current of truth.

Something made Jimmy take another look at "Elvis has left the building." It jumped out at him. Captain Rick was the biggest fan of The King that he knew, and that was well known. The coded message made sense to him, now. Jimmy's realization that his captain was out there somewhere gave a much needed jolt to his flagging morale.

Despite the propaganda and the government filters and the snooping by the government's agents, the internet was just too vast and too complex to lock down. Blatantly shutting it off entirely would be such a vulgar display of tyranny that to do so would cause more trouble than it was worth. Even the Chinese wouldn't go that far. An operational internet actually served the government as both an anger-venting mechanism for the proles — talking about it usually replaces doing it — and also for monitoring anti-patriots who unintentionally out themselves. The feds intended to leave the internet partially on until the costs began to exceed the benefits.

Marzan went back through the forum posts. *'Lucifer Rising...'* *What does that mean? Lucifer is the morning star — Venus. What is Venus? Is it something evil? Something bright? Fast moving?*

Marzan knew he couldn't stay with Vaughn much longer. He was waiting for leadership and it now appeared that it was out there waiting for him. He hoped to stick around long enough to at least help get Vaughn back to sanity, but he wasn't hopeful. Vaughn was deteriorating by the hour. He was becoming the undead. Marzan had seen the undead before.

Marzan heard a truck slowing to make the turn onto Vaughn's driveway.

"Shit! Someone's coming!" he shouted as he grabbed his rifle and made his way to the back room. He had assembled a darkened perch in there which provided a decent vantage over the driveway and down into the woods. The window was fully open, even in the bitter cold. A fully open window is half as obvious as a half open one.

An old Sierra pickup rolled down Vaughn's driveway. It bore no resemblance to any kind of cop car, undercover or otherwise. It lacked the giveaway antennae. "It's the kidnappers or a messenger I bet," Vaughn shouted.

The truck parked at the driveway's end, its engine left running. The driver door opened.

"If they're cops, they are really stupid," Marzan remarked. "I could smoke 'em all in three seconds."

A small Latino man stepped out of the rusted truck. He was wearing a puffy winter coat that bloused out as he raised his tattooed hands in the air. He stood next to the truck with his bare hands raised.

"Who are you?" Vaughn shouted out the door.

"I'm unarmed," he shouted back. He did a slow pirouette, then walked carefully down the driveway towards Vaughn's front door, hands still raised.

"You got my wife?" Vaughn shouted back.

"I need to talk. You come outside. Okay? There's not much time."

"Where's my wife?" Vaughn shouted again.

Marzan snapped his fingers at Vaughn from down the hall to get his attention. "I've got you covered," Marzan whispered. He gave

Vaughn a thumbs-up and clicked the safety off his M4. He aimed. "Just like Shariastan," he mumbled.

Marzan was cloaked in the darkness of the room. The visitors, which included three others in the front seat of the Sierra, would not be able to see him. Their heads panned behind the windshield, searching for spotters or snipers. Vaughn took a deep breath and went out the door. He walked cautiously down the steps and approached the visitor standing in the driveway.

"Do I know you?" Vaughn asked.

"You call me Joe Joe," he answered.

"Do I know you?"

"We met before," he answered, hands still raised.

"Where?"

"I was the one who broke in your house that night. You stop me with your gun."

Vaughn lost his words for a moment as he looked Joe Joe over.

"But I come here and help you," Joe Joe added.

"What did you do to my wife?" he shouted, balling his fists.

"Nothing. I swear. But I help you. You to listen to me."

"Want me to smoke him, Vaughn?" Marzan shouted from the house. Guns clicked inside the Sierra as the three silhouetted faces inside ducked and raised their guns towards Marzan's voice emanating from the open window.

"Please! Please!" Joe Joe pleaded. "I am unarmed. I help you." He turned to the truck and shouted, Bajen sus armas!"

"Where's my wife?" Vaughn asked again.

"Look," Joe Joe continued, "you a good man. You could have kill me that night but you didn't. I owe you for that."

"Why are you here?"

"I tell you something, okay?"

"You tell me where my wife is."

"I no take her, okay? But I know where she is."

"You tell me right now or I'll tell my friend back there to waste all you motherfuckers."

"Please listen. We no shoot. You a good man. I no take her but I know where she is. I know who take her. It's not me. But I know who."

"Tell me then!"

Joe Joe kept his hands up. They were turning purple from the cold. "Listen," his eyes widened with a pleading expression. A white vapor plume escaped through his silvery dental work with each exhale.

Marzan's crosshair was locked on to Joe Joe's head. One smooth

146

squeeze, a jolt, and Joe Joe's skull would burst apart out the back. Then Marzan would swing the rifle into the Sierra's windshield and empty his magazine. He hoped Vaughn had enough sense to take cover.

"You listen, okay?" Joe Joe continued. "No shoot me. Tell that man in house, 'no shoot', okay?" Joe Joe waited for Vaughn to give the order. "You tell him 'no shoot' and I tell you where your wife is."

"All right." Vaughn turned to the window. "Don't shoot unless something happens to me."

Marzan didn't answer.

"He hear you?" Joe Joe asked.

"He isn't deaf."

"Okay. We want no trouble."

"Tell me where she is."

Joe Joe slowly lowered his hands. "I reach in my pocket. Okay with you?"

"Go slow."

Joe Joe reached his right hand into his pocket and slowly withdrew it. He handed Vaughn a silvery object and Vaughn took it from him to inspect it.

"What is it?" Marzan shouted through the window.

"It's her wedding ring," Vaughn answered. "Where'd you get it?" he asked Joe Joe.

"I know a pawnbroker. He my medio hermano. He there, in the truck."

"Why would he care?" Vaughn asked, trying to pick him out from the three ducking silhouettes in the cab.

"Because he know it's your wife."

"How would he know?"

"We know everything that happen up here in your mountain town. We know everything. The one that clean your house, the one that cook your meal, the one that mow your lawn, they our sister and brother and cousin and uncle and aunt. They see. They hear. They tell. They know everything. We know everything. I'm in a crew. Knowing is our job. We know everything that happen up here. We know about your wife, Mr. Clayton. We know she was kidnap."

"But why? Why would he care? Why would you care?"

"Because the man who pawn it. I know — we all know who he is. He an evil man."

"Who is he?"

"He a cop. But he no normal cop. Most cop are okay. They do their job. They bust you for this, they bust you for that, but they follow the rule. This cop, he no follow the rule. He Taser one. He Taser another. He shake some down. He torture some for nothing. He torture me. He bust my hand. He try to rape me. He a drunk. He drunk on power. He a fucking pendejo."

"Who is he?"

"His name is Bob Garrity. He sell this ring to my medio hermano for silver coins. He dumb. He don't know who my brother is. My brother ask, 'where you get this ring?' Garrity lie. He say he stole it but if he stole it, he wouldn't say that. My brother figure it out. He tell me all about it when I get out. We come here and show you the ring. Now I know he the one. He kidnap your wife."

"Sounds like he's trying to get you to do his dirty work," Marzan shouted.

"I no have anyone do my dirty work," said Joe Joe.

"Why are you here, then?" asked Marzan.

"Because I wrong this man," Joe Joe shouted back, looking directly into Vaughn's eyes. "It's my fault your wife is kidnap—my fault. Garrity think I come here for your gold coin. But I was wrong. I was wrong and now your wife is kidnap by that psycho. Now I come here and make it right. Here, you take this..." Joe Joe reached in his pocket and produced a business card which he handed to Vaughn.

"Whose number is this?"

"That Bob Garrity's nomber. He give that card to me. That address, he live there. I wrote that there for you."

Vaughn and Joe Joe stared into each other's eyes.

"You go see him. You go see Bob Garrity. You find out for yourself. But go soon, before it's too late. Your wife, she no last long. Bob Garrity—he no last long either," Joe Joe spat.

"Why? You planning on doing something?"

"No, not me. We're leaving. He have all the enemy he need. Even the cop want him dead. I just want you to get your wife back. She a good mother. I remember she say for you to shoot me. That's a good mother. I want you to get her back. Jesus, he see everything. I try to make it right. You go see that fat pig Bob Garrity. He have your wife."

"Where're you going?"

"I going home, home to El Salvador. We leave this country right now, right from here. Your Amerika is finished."

Chapter 22

"Calm down a second," Jimmy begged.

Vaughn was manically scurrying around the house, not exactly sure what he was going to do but desperately wanting to get on with doing it.

Jimmy grabbed him by the shoulder. "Vaughn, you need to think about this for a second."

Vaughn stopped.

"Are you sure this gangbanger is telling the truth?"

"Yes, I'm sure. It all makes sense. If he wanted me to cap the sheriff he'd just say that Jess was dead."

"What if you're wrong?"

"I'm not wrong." Vaughn shrugged off Jimmy's grasp. "I have to go get her."

"So what's your plan, then? What are you going to do? How are you going to do it?"

"I'm going over there and hold that bastard at gunpoint until I get her back."

"Oh, just like that? It's that simple? Think, Vaughn. What if you go over there, all guns-a-blazin', and it turns out she's not there. Then what? They might hurt her, Vaughn. You might never get her back then."

"I can't just sit around here."

"You need a plan. You need to write it all down. Map it out. Your goal is to find out where she is. You need to figure out how you're going to get that information. Then you need to figure out how you're going to get her back safely. And on top of all that, you need to figure out how to do it without getting hurt, yourself. This guy is a sheriff. He's a professional."

Vaughn clenched his fists. "What do you suggest?" he snapped.

Marzan walked over to the sink while scratching his head. He took a glass from the cupboard and filled it with water and took a long drink. He paused.

"What is it?" Vaughn asked.

Marzan labored deep in thought for a few seconds. He rubbed his head and looked at the half-empty glass. "This is a complicated situation for a civilian like you, but not so complicated for me." There was nothing in it for Jimmy Marzan to help Vaughn other than his own redemption. He wasn't even sure if it would accomplish that; redemption is so difficult to quantify. "Before we do anything, you need to make sure you know what you're getting into, Vaughn. You need to know that there is no turning back from this. You need to be fully committed."

"I understand."

"You need to know that...well...you need to understand that it might be...that it might actually be too late to do anything."

"What do you mean?"

"I'm not saying that it *is* too late. I'm just saying that you haven't heard anything from the kidnappers for a few days now. You have to be prepared for all possibilities. If the worst-case scenario has happened, how will you respond to that? You won't be able to think about it rationally when you're in the middle of it. You won't have time to sort through the emotions. You have to decide that now, before you go."

"I'll kill him then."

"Make sure you are not rash about this, Vaughn. You really have to think this all the way through. It's easy to say this or that, here and now, but out there it's different. I'm not saying you'll freeze up or anything. It's hard to know that in advance. I'm just saying you need to decide what you'll do before you get out there in the middle of it. You have to commit to a plan right now."

"Do you know what this will bring down on you, Vaughn? Do you intend to get away with it or do you even care? What about your daughter? Your daughter needs her father, Vaughn. These are really tough times. If the worst-case scenario has happened, and you go for payback and you end up getting caught or killed, who will raise your daughter? Are you prepared to ask yourself these questions? Think it all the way through."

"If Jessica's dead, I want him dead. My life won't matter anymore."

Marzan was tuned to the devil speaking with Vaughn's tongue and seeing with Vaughn's eyes. Jimmy had been there himself, but that was in a warzone 10,000 miles away. Being in a war somehow legitimized it. Or did it?

"Are you sure you don't want to go to the police?"

"C'mon, Jimmy."

"I just want to make sure."

"The kidnapper is the police."

"Maybe you could go to the FBI or something."

"It's chaos out there. They're not going to help me."

"Okay. I just had to ask one more time. But I want you to let me help you."

"No. This isn't your problem."

"It is my problem, Vaughn. I believe in fate. I believe fate put me here. You helped me and now I've got to help you. I've done things like this before. I can help but you must trust me. You have to do things my way. Do you understand?"

"I appreciate that. But I—"

"I mean it. My way. If you trust me then we'll both get what we want."

"Okay."

"Do you trust me, Vaughn?"

"I do."

"Are you certain?"

"Yes. What do we need to do?"

"First, we need to find out what this Garrity knows."

"And how do we do that?"

"We need to ask him."

"And what if he won't answer?"

"Then I'll use my expertise in the art of persuasion."

Vaughn parked the truck and he and Marzan started on a half-mile hike over the crusty snow through the pine trees toward Garrity's house. It was 3:01 a.m. and it was a crystal-clear, moonless night, bitter and frigid and still. They walked as quietly as they could and didn't speak except in faint whispers.

Marzan scanned the terrain with his night vision for anyone who might be a sentry or a witness. He thought of the insurgents back in Shariastan who quickly figured out how to evade the Americans' night-eyes. Leaves and twigs woven into natural fibers reduced their contrast and concealed them from night vision. Covering their faces and wearing rubber boots and leather belts and sheathing their gun barrels with cotton socks and t shirts made them almost invisible to infrared. Warfare promotes a sort of violent, accelerated Darwinism. The most adaptable, clever, and ruthless survive to pass their knowledge on. The thoughtless and unlucky are removed from the gene pool.

Jimmy assumed that the expanding force of American insurgents would soon figure out how to survive their occupiers as well. It would be a brutal process of adapting to technological disadvantage, but there is always a window of opportunity early on, when the occupier's hubris renders him inattentive.

The only movement in the frozen night was that of the ghostlike plumes of chimney smoke floating silently upwards and dissolving into the stars.

Vaughn stopped. "That has to be it," he whispered, pointing to the giant cabin fifty yards off through the trees. A lone exterior light shined above the garage. Marzan scanned the windows with his optics. They were all black, curtains drawn.

"I wonder if he has dogs," Marzan asked.

"Good question."

"Let's assume he does."

"What do we do, then?"

"We use them."

Marzan explained tactics to Vaughn and the two split up with Vaughn making a wide arc to the south of the house. He waited there, hidden in the brambles at the base of an ancient ponderosa tree. After exactly fifteen minutes, he hurled a snowball at the house. Nothing happened. He threw another, this time aiming for a window. He ducked back into the brush after the throw. Again, nothing. Another. Nothing. *No dogs,* he thought. *Better try a couple more times just to be sure.* He probed through the snow for a stone or something but came up with nothing more substantial than a handful of pine cones. He looked around again and then up into the tree. He grabbed hold of a dead branch and snapped it off. *One more try,* he thought. He took a deep breath and hurled the stick into the house and dove back into the shrubs. That did the trick. Two big dogs barked, rabidly. They burst out of a doggy door and darted into the yard where they continued barking blindly at whatever was lurking in the night.

Marzan stealthily made his way into the house through a garage window and was waiting patiently in the darkness when he heard the dogs. He followed their barking to the doggy door, which he blocked off on the inside by pushing an armchair up against it. He prayed there wasn't another door that would let them back in as they sounded like big enough dogs to take him down.

Come on. Wake up, Garrity, Marzan thought. He scanned the

house with his optics, switching from starlight to infrared beam, as there was not enough ambient light to illuminate anything. He was in a lower-level recreation room of some sort judging by the pool table. He squeezed into a corner listening for any footfalls. The dogs continued barking outside. *Come on, wake up.*

"God damn it!" shouted someone upstairs. "Daisy! Stossi! Shut up!"

Thunk.

Lumbering footfalls stumbled across the ceiling over Marzan's head. They paused at the south end of the house. Marzan deduced that Garrity was looking out a window. It was the perfect moment.

Marzan drew his 9mm with silencer attached, took a glance through his optics to get his bearings, then moved silently up the staircase. Once at the top, he looked into living room area. He saw nothing for a moment. He was tempted to use his optics again, but then, as his eyes adjusted, he spotted the silhouette of a large-framed man at a window peering out between the curtains towards the barking.

His moment of opportunity had come. Marzan had to move.

Quickly, silently, he darted into the living room right up behind the unaware and half-asleep undersheriff and placed the barrel of his pistol against the base of his skull.

"Do not move. Do not speak," Marzan whispered calmly. "Put your hands up."

Garrity complied.

"Come with me quietly if you want to live."

Marzan backed him slowly away from the window, across the room, and down the stairs.

"What do you want?" Garrity asked.

"I'll be asking the questions. Do not speak unless spoken too. If you speak without being spoken to you will feel pain."

Marzan marched Garrity into the garage where he switched on a dangling light bulb.

"Unfold that chair over there. Good. Now take a seat."

Garrity, clad only in his boxer briefs, sat down in the frozen chair. "Do you know who I am?" Garrity asked.

"Go ahead and tell me."

"I'm a sheriff. My name is Bob Garrity. And you're making a big mistake coming here. What gang are you with?"

"That's enough."

Marzan dialed Vaughn on his cell. "I've got him in the garage.

Yeah, it's him. Hurry up. Come in through the window on the north side." He hung up.

Marzan and Garrity stared at each other, Marzan standing, dressed in black, bank-robber-style stocking cap pulled over his face, 9mm in his hand. Garrity sitting, nearly naked, flabby white skin folding over the waistband of his shorts.

"You're not a gangbanger, are you?" Garrity asked.

"What makes you ask that?"

"Because you don't hold your gun sideways. You wield it like a pro."

"You are correct. I'm no gangbanger."

"Are you sure you know who I am?" Garrity asked again.

"You've confirmed it for me. Now, shut the fuck up."

Vaughn appeared, crawling through the window with a rustle, clumsily carrying his shotgun. He knocked the snow off his sleeves once inside.

"Here," Vaughn said, "You take my pistol and keep it pointed — right at his chest. If he makes any rapid movements, shoot him two times. Then put another round in his head point blank." Marzan handed Vaughn the 9mm and reached into his pocket for a spool of kite string. He used it to tie up Garrity's wrists.

"Where's my wife?" Vaughn asked, pointing the gun with a shaky grip.

"I'll ask the questions," Marzan said. "You just hold the gun." Marzan lashed and tied off Garrity's joints to the flimsy chair. The string cut into Garrity's skin and cut off his circulation. Marzan pulled Garrity's ankles and elbows into unnatural angles. Both of his elbows were cinched inwards towards the chest. His knees were drawn together but his ankles were spread apart with his feet lifted off the floor. His left wrist and most of his hand was lashed to the armrest with his palm down. Garrity grimaced in pain.

"I'm a sheriff! I..."

Marzan smothered Garrity's face with his hand and pressed his thumb into Garrity's left eye socket. He pushed it in deeply, pushing his eyeball into his skull.

Garrity growled.

"I told you twice already to shut up. I warned you that you would feel pain if you didn't. Keep it up and you'll be made to feel blindness too. Do you understand me?"

"Yes. Okay."

Marzan finished the lashing and knotting and tying. When

complete, Garrity was completely immobilized and resembled an insect wound up in a spider's cocoon.

"Is there anyone else here?" Marzan asked.

Garrity shook his head.

Marzan turned to Vaughn, "He's a liar. I want you to check out the house. Then find the bathroom. Take those two buckets with you and fill them up with water. Don't turn on too many lights."

"What if I find someone up there?"

"Tell them they won't be harmed if they cooperate. Then bring them down here so we can keep an eye on them. If they resist or run, shoot them, but try to shoot them below the knee."

Vaughn left with the buckets and carrying the pistol. He left the shotgun with Jimmy.

"Now for you," Marzan continued, "I have some questions for you, sheriff. Hmmm. But before we get started...let's have a look at what we have here."

Marzan stepped over to a toolbox on a workbench and fumbled around in it with one hand. He intentionally jingled the tools about, making as much clanging noise as possible. A screwdriver fell out onto the floor. Marzan picked it up and drove its tip into the wooden workbench so that it stood upright. He continued digging. "What might this be good for?" he asked, as he revealed a pair of Vice-Grips. He squeezed the squeaky handle a few times in front of Garrity's face. "Looks like something I could use to pull teeth. Do you like your teeth, Bob? You can answer."

Garrity nodded affirmatively.

"What else do we have?" Marzan produced a rubber mallet. "Now what could I do with this? I wonder. Hmmm." He slammed the hammer down on the bench. Garrity winced at the sound. "I imagine I could pretty much hammer someone's balls flat with one of these. What do you think, Bob?"

"Yes. Yes you could."

"What else is in here?"

Clang. Thud. Ping.

Marzan pulled out a set of needle-nose pliers. "Interesting. I could twist someone's nipples clean off with this."

"I'm sure," Garrity answered. "Please, I don't know what you want but I can get you — "

"Shut up!"

Marzan used the pliers to take hold of Garrity's ear lobe, squeezing it as tight as he could without breaking the skin. Garrity howled.

Marzan spoke calmly. "You have some information for us and you're going to give it up tonight."

"What...what do you want?"

Marzan released the pliers. He looked around the garage again. He found an ice cooler under the bench. He slid it along the floor, stopping it just at Garrity's feet. He grabbed a handful of instruments from the toolbox and set them on the lid of the cooler, aligning them as if he were about to perform surgery. Garrity started to shiver. Marzan held up the locking pliers again and slowly turned the thumb crank back and forth in front of Garrity's eyes.

Vaughn finally returned with the buckets.

"You weren't gone very long," Marzan said. "Did you check the whole house? Anyone else inside?"

"Nobody else here. Just the dogs outside."

"Where's my gun?"

"It's in my belt."

Good. Now, for you..."

Marzan found a rag on a shelf and soaked it in the water of one of the buckets. Then he stuffed it into Garrity's mouth. Garrity's eyes widened as Marzan approached him with a blindfold.

"Give me a hand," he said to Vaughn.

They tipped Garrity's chair backward so that his hairy, bare back was resting on the chair back and the cold concrete floor. "Take the 9mm out," Marzan said to Vaughn. Marzan set down the shotgun and picked up the bucket of water. He poured a stream onto the rag stuffed in Garrity's mouth. The water splashed over his face and travelled up his nostrils. He reflexively tried to hold his breath but the droplets of water trickled into his sinuses triggering his exhale and cough reflexes. Garrity couldn't breathe. Marzan stopped after about ten seconds. He took the rag out.

"Now," Marzan explained softly, "you are going to tell us where is Jessica Clayton?"

"I don't—"

Before Garrity could even complete his denial, Marzan shoved the rag back in his mouth and proceeded to pour another stream of water up into his nostrils. This time, he did it for about thirty seconds before stopping.

"Okay," Marzan said calmly, "I'm going to ask you again, where is Jessica Clayton? But before you answer, I'm going to ask Jessica's husband over there to go get that hammer ready. Vaughn, please get that mallet right there and prepare to flatten Bob's testicles. Oh, and when I turn you loose, don't hold anything back."

Vaughn grabbed the hammer and was about to let loose —

"Please, I..." Garrity pleaded.

Marzan stayed Vaughn and stuffed the rag back Garity's mouth and poured the water again. Vaughn stood anxiously with the mallet in one hand and the 9mm in the other. He knew that he had to control his rage or he would never find out where Jessica was.

Marzan poured and Garrity coughed and squealed and choked. Marzan kept pouring until the bucket was out of water. Then he calmly set the empty pail down. The frigid air of the garage combined with the cold water drew most of the heat out of Garrity's body. He started shivering violently. Steam wafted off him. Marzan took the rag out of his mouth again.

"Okay," Marzan continued, "are you ready to cooperate or do I need to turn him loose with that mallet?"

"I don't know —"

Marzan shoved the rag back in and began to pour the second bucket. Vaughn stepped forward with the hammer in his hand and the devil in his eyes but Marzan looked him back. He poured for over a minute as Garrity coughed and choked. Marzan set the bucket down and took the rag out of Garrity's mouth once more.

"You better wise up, Bob. Because when this bucket runs out of water, I'll have no choice but to turn him loose. I'm not kidding. Do you understand? We could fuck you up real good."

"Y...y...yes. I do. I'll tell you."

Marzan stood up surprised. He didn't expect Garrity to give up so easily. They were much tougher back in Shariastan. "Excellent," he answered. "So tell us then. Where is Jessica Clayton?"

"Are you going to kill me?" Garrity asked.

Marzan shoved the rag back into Bob's mouth and started pouring the water again. But only a short pour was necessary this time. "My water is running low, Bob. When it runs out, we will begin the process of busting your balls.." Garrity shook his head and coughed, spraying droplets of ice water everywhere.

"Tell me Bob, where is Jessica Clayton?"

"Okay! I'll tell you," Garrity sobbed.

"Excellent. Now just wait a second..." Marzan interrupted, turning to Vaughn. "Help me tilt him up."

Vaughn helped lift Garrity's chair and shivering body upright.

"Get your camera ready," Marzan ordered.

Marzan set the hammer down and took his cell phone out of his pocket. He turned on the video recorder. The first image he captured was of Marzan pulling Bob's blindfold off.

"Okay," Marzan narrated, "we are conducting an interview of Sheriff — or is it Undersheriff? — Bob Garrity. We are in his garage. After enhanced interrogation, Bob has decided to cooperate by answering our questions. Okay, Bob. Tell us, what did you do with Jessica Clayton?"

Bob stammered and coughed. Marzan reached over and gabbed the hammer to remind Bob of what he was in for if he didn't answer. Garrity lowered his head and wept. Vaughn captured his steaming head bobbing with each pathetic sob. Garrity was shivering uncontrollably and his skin was beginning to turn bluish white.

"Bob!" Marzan shouted. "Bob! Answer the question, Bob. Where is Jessica Clayton?"

Garrity moaned. The twine was shrinking with the cold moisture and drawing tight around his joints, turning his skin purple.

"Bob, this is your last chance." Marzan slammed the hammer down into his palm. *Crack. Crack. Crack.*

"She's..." Garrity stuttered.

"Yes?"

"...She's at a campground. She's at a campground."

"Where?" Vaughn shouted, nearly dropping his phone.

"She's at the campground on the road from Wellington Lake back to Buffalo Creek. You'll see it off on the north side. Site 21. It's the only site with an outhouse out there. They just built it last summer. It hasn't been used yet."

"It's freezing out there."

"She's underground."

"Is she dead?" Vaughn screamed. "Is she dead? If she's dead I'll shoot you right here!" Vaughn shook the 9mm in Garrity's face. "Is she dead? Answer me!"

"No! Sh...she's underground. She has a propane heater. She has water. She's got blankets. Please don't kill me. I didn't hurt her. I didn't know what I was doing. I...I was insane. I was going to release her after the storm cleared. Please. I just want to get out of here. I just want to get out of the country. I'll take you to her. Please, just don't kill me."

"Shut up," Marzan barked. He held Vaughn back. He was gripping the 9mm so tightly that his knuckles whitened. "Easy there, Vaughn. Jessica is our priority."

"What do we do with him? Bring him along?"

"No way. If we get stopped with him we're finished. And if we're finished then Jessica's finished, too."

"We can't just leave him. He'll go for help. Can you stay here and watch him?"

"We should stay together. It might take two of us to get her out."

"Then what do we do? Kill him?"

"Put that camera away. Hand me your shotgun."

"No!" Garrity pleaded. "No! No! Don't kill me. No! I didn't hurt her. I just..."

Vaughn stashed his phone, reached down to pick up his shotgun and handed it to Marzan. Jimmy walked over to the workbench and set it into a swivel vise. Once the stock was gripped firmly between the jaws, he tied a slipknot into the end of his twine and looped it tight over the trigger. Then he ran the line back under the crank on the vise, up over three rafters above and back down to the floor. They moved Garrity in the chair so his chest was facing directly into the barrel of the shotgun with the string dangling down from the ceiling at his wrist. Marzan grabbed the hammer and tied the end of the dangling string to it, making sure that all the slack was pulled out. Then he put the hammer in Garrity's left hand. He could barely hold it in his purple fingers.

"Go find Bob some blankets or something."

Vaughn left but quickly returned with two coats which he placed over Garrity's shivering body. Then Marzan chambered a shell in the shotgun.

"There," he said, as he plucked the taut line. "Hang on to that hammer, my friend. If you let it go, the tension in that line will yank the trigger and go boom. We're going to get Jessica. If we find her, we'll come back with the police. But if we get out there and we can't find her or she's — you know — then we'll be coming back for you. Do you understand? We'll be coming back for you and the misery and pain you will suffer in the few remaining moments of your life will be beyond the realm of human comprehension. So if you have anything else you want to tell us, tell us now. This is your last chance."

"She's there. You'll find her."

Marzan gagged him with one of the dog's tennis balls and a strip of duct tape. Then he clicked the safety off on the shotgun. He asked Vaughn for his 9mm back.

"Where are you going?" Vaughn asked.

"I've got to go take care of the dogs."

159

Chapter 23

Mae made herself as small and quiet as she could in the back corner of the bedroom closet, using the hanging clothes as extra cover. The dogs barked and barked outside. She couldn't understand why they weren't charging back into the house. They should be tearing apart the intruder that had taken Bob downstairs.

Bob kept a revolver in his nightstand but Mae had no idea how to use it. She had never fired a gun before. It had hammers and safeties and unfamiliar, dangerous mechanisms to worry about. Even if she did know how to wield it, she lacked the fortitude to act decisively on the intruder. She worried he might see her first and blow her away before she could overcome her hesitancy.

She was petrified of the demon in the darkness. He was undoubtedly an expert in the way he had so quickly, silently, and effortlessly subdued a professional law enforcer. She tried not to breathe too loud.

Footsteps, she silently screamed in her mind. *Please don't come in here.*

The footsteps stopped at the bedroom door.

Oh God. Please no. Don't come in here. Please. Please.

She heard the door handle turn and then the door sweep open across the carpet and into the dark bedroom. She heard Bob's screams from downstairs. He seemed so far away.

Click.

A sliver of light appeared under the closet door. She noticed the calf of her leg was exposed, sticking out from behind the hanging blind of clothes. She drew it back into her body slowly.

Please don't...please don't look in here, she pleaded silently.

Click.

The sliver of light vanished. The footsteps made their way back down the hall and into the bathroom. Mae heard the tub faucet turn on. She sighed.

There must have been at least two intruders, because she could hear Bob's screams and pleas directed at one of them in the downstairs garage while the other worked the faucet in the upstairs bath. The knobs squeaked. The water stopped. The footsteps left the bathroom and made their way back down the stairs.

She waited quietly in the darkness, petrified that there might be a third intruder waiting silently in the room, waiting patiently for her to peek her face out of the closet and snatch her by the hair and drag her outside where some unknown, hellish fate awaited. She waited in the darkness.

She heard Bob coughing. She heard the muffled voices of the intruders. *Who are they? Gangbangers? Kidnappers?* Maybe they were parolees using the cover of chaos to take revenge on the cop who had put them away in the past.

After a while, it seemed safe for Mae to peek out. She slowly, quietly opened the closet door and poked her head out into the pitch-black room. She opened the door further, carefully, just wide enough to crawl out. To her relief, no one was there waiting to grab her by the scalp. But her heart still raced.

She crawled over to the nightstand and got Bob's revolver. The weight and unwieldiness of it surprised her. She sat Indian style on the floor, next to the nightstand, holding the gun, back against the bed, wearing nothing but a t-shirt.

She tried to muster some courage. If she dialed the cops, it would take them at least twenty minutes to get to Bob's secluded house. And that was if they answered at all. 9-1-1 was only sporadically available. And if she called, the intruders might hear her. And she couldn't find the phone in the darkness anyway. And she dared not turn on the light. So she took a long deep breath and pulled herself up onto her feet holding the gun.

She clasped the revolver with both hands as she carefully stepped out of the bedroom and proceeded down the stairs, then around a corner to the door leading into the garage. She could hear the intruder's voices clearly. She heard water and coughing. It was Bob's coughing.

What are they doing to him? she asked herself.

The intruders were just behind the door, just a few feet away. She heard splashing, wheezing, and threatening commands. If she could just open the door and point the gun at them then Bob would take it from there. *But they have guns, too,* she considered. *They'll shoot me dead. No, I can't do it. I can't.* She couldn't open the door.

Terror coursed through her arteries, freezing her in fear. Her hands clumsily clutched the gun with its heavy barrel pointed droopily towards the door. She thought for a second about just pulling the trigger and hoping the explosion might be enough to scare them off. No, that was too risky. She didn't even have the nerve to put her finger on the trigger. She remained frozen.

She heard one of the invaders speak. "Bob, this is your last chance." *Crack. Crack. Crack.* "She's..." Garrity stuttered, "She's at a campground. She's at a campground."

What does that mean? Who was at a campground? She asked herself. She could hardly believe her ears when she heard the rest of Bob's confession. She wanted to throw the gun down and run out into the snow. But for a moment she rationalized it. *There's no way Bob could do such a thing,* she assured herself. But she quickly overcame this thought as well. It was true. She knew Bob's truth when he told it.

Who was this woman? What did Bob do to her? Why did he do this? The money? Was it for traveling money to get us to Costa Rica?

Her instinct for self-preservation suddenly manifested itself. She knew that she would most certainly be implicated in Bob's scheme and, at the very least, her career would be ruined by such a scandal. She hobnobbed with the Treasury secretary's family and the president's Cabinet and all those billionaire bankers and their Botoxed, Long Island wives. She relished that life—the travel, the money, the cocktail parties where the patricians bitched about their lawsuits and their detached, rotten kids. *This is not happening!* Her life would be destroyed by this scandal. She couldn't just surrender it over Bob's stupidity. She would be ruined. Her career would, at best, be relegated to some mahogany hall in some bland, multinational corporate office. It would be a living hell, wasting her days and remaining vitality cooking up financial lies and P&L propaganda for some Eau Claire, cheddar-cheese conglomerate. She'd almost rather blow her brains out right then and there. She looked down at the gun in her hand.

Stop thinking like a loser, she cajoled herself. *You will not accept this. You cannot allow yourself to be tied to this scandal. This is Bob's mess, let him deal with it. You have to go! Go now! Run! Run!*

But she couldn't. She heard the invader's footsteps. She held the gun up. She placed her two manicured index fingers on the trigger. Now she was ready, ready to shoot. She would shoot them and make Bob clean it all up and then she would leave him for good. She never should have come back anyway. *He's a loser,* she thought, *a redneck, loser undersheriff in a hick county in a fly-over state.*

A set of footsteps went out the side door of the garage. Then the interior garage door opened. Mae pointed the gun. A figure appeared before her but it wasn't Bob. It was an intruder. He stood in the frame of the door like a wraith, a shadow backlit by the orange glow of Hades. He mechanically raised his 9mm to her forehead. She

163

feebly, shakily, raised Bob's revolver in defense. Their eyes met. But Mae could not squeeze the trigger. A flash, a final instant of existence, and she would be no more. She lowered the pistol and dropped her eyes and shook her head. She was beaten...finished.

But Jimmy Marzan left her there and slipped into the backyard.

She waited for a moment, listening to Bob sobbing in the garage. She stepped through the doorway. She found Bob covered with coats, blindfolded and gagged and soaking wet and shivering. She approached him, gun in hand. He didn't hear her. He was just trying to breathe through the gag.

"How could you do this?" she asked him.

Bob mumbled through the tennis ball and duct tape.

Instinctively, she pulled the hammer back on the pistol, like she had seen in movies so many times. "How could you do this to me?" she screamed.

Bob mumbled and strained under his gag and restraints. His coats fell off revealing his bindings. Bob gripped the mallet tied to the trigger of the shotgun tightly in his frozen hand. Mae ripped his blindfold off. Bob screamed muffled screams, but she didn't remove the gag. She just stood with the gun, hammer cocked, directly between Bob's knotted, shivering body and the shotgun affixed to the vice that was aimed at his chest. The dogs barked viciously outside. Bob shook his head vehemently from side to side, trying to use his eyes to direct her to the shotgun.

"No! Be careful. Don't touch that string! Take this gag off. Look! Look behind you!" But his gagged pleas were unintelligible.

"You bastard!" she said, raising the barrel to his face.

No, Mae. No. I did it for us. I did it for you. I love you.

Her shoulder pressed up against the string tied to the trigger. The line drew taut. Bob tried to raise the mallet up in his hand to put more slack in the line but his knots had little give left in them. He held his breath. The dogs snarled and growled away in the yard. He looked into her eyes. He saw only ice.

He prayed. He prayed that the all-consuming obsession he had for her — far more for her than for any other in all his life — would mean something to her now. She was angelic in his mind, a powerful woman, a woman of crystalline intellect and shrewdness and class. Mae, with her razor sharp edges and impenetrable armor, a woman so desirable, so feminine and beautiful and perfect — he prayed that she might finally know him now. She must understand him after all this. She must comprehend his ruthlessness. She must know that he was just like

164

her, that they were the same, that they were made for each other. She had to know this now. She had to love him now. They were of one mind and one spirit. He had finally proven his worthiness. He had finally proven his devotion to her by the lengths he was willing to go.

He looked into her eyes. *They will soften,* he hoped. *She will throw down the gun and embrace me and press herself against me and become one with me.* He had finally conquered the unconquerable Maiden Lane. He had finally made her love him.

But no.

No, she did not love him. Her cold, cat's-eye stare revealed that. He saw nothing in her glassy eyes but contempt. *No. No. No.* he cried inside. He had failed. He had failed to win her again.

He was going to drop the mallet, drop the mallet and kill her with a shotgun blast. She would drop into his arms and he would be, if not immersed in an embrace of her love, at least awash in her blood. No, there was no trace of love in her eyes for him. He knew it was finally over. So many years of his life wasted chasing her and trying to prove himself to her and to win her back. It was time to drop the hammer.

Drop it!

But he couldn't do that either. He held on. He was pathetic.

His beloved shepherds ceased their barking. He loved those dogs but now they were dead and gone. Soon Mae would be gone and he would be alone again. And if he survived the cold he would be arrested or perhaps worse.

Mae stepped back and the slack in the string returned.

"Don't go," he mumbled through the gag in futility.

But Mae pulled away from him, leaving him knotted up in the frozen garage.

"No. Don't go, Mae. I love you," he sobbed.

But she left him there and went back into the house. She came back one last time, dressed and with a bag. He knew she was too meticulous to leave anything behind. She threw the bag into Bob's truck. Then she looked at him one last time. Bob hoped that maybe she would change her mind. He prayed that she would come to her senses and at least untie him. He wanted nothing in life other than to be near her, to hold her, if only for a few fleeting moments. But he knew by her expression that she was leaving and would not be coming back.

Mae never changed her mind. He realized then that she didn't come back for him anyway. She was just using him. She turned off the garage light and got into his truck and started it up. The light came back on again when she opened the garage door and drove his truck off into the cold night.

Bob imagined himself discovered frozen to death. It was no matter. Everything was lost for him. Even if the brotherhood covered for him, which they probably wouldn't, they would not be able to restore his life from the ruined state it was in. *And why would they, anyway?* he asked himself. He couldn't breathe. It was as if one of the intruders had taken the mallet and hammered him in the diaphragm. He struggled against the knots but it was hopeless.

My dogs, he wept. Poor Daisy. Poor Stossi. My angels. They held my life together when Mae left the first time. My glorious, loyal shepherds are dead." He had seen many dead dogs. He imagined them lying on their sides in the snow, tongues hanging out, blank eyes stuck open.

What is my life worth anymore? What am I worth as a man? I can't even run. I'm penniless. I'm trapped. I'm alone. I'm naked tied to a folding chair. I have a shotgun pointed at my heart and a trigger tied to a hammer in my numb hand. How will I be found? If they find me alive, what will I say? The intruders had filmed his confession so it was pointless to attempt to contrive a story. He was finished any way he looked at it.

He began shivering uncontrollably. Soon, the hypothermia would put him to sleep. His hand would relax. The hammer would fall out. The shotgun would fire. He would be dead. The pain would be over. Bob Garrity looked into the barrel of the shotgun. He gazed down at the hammer in his hand. He prayed it would be instantaneous. The timer ran out and the garage light switched off.

Two hours later, Mae passed into the federal bunker complex at Denver International. She told T what had happened. T had Bob's truck hauled away to be destroyed. Two escorts took Mae down into the catacombs, there. The red door appeared once again before her. She stepped forward and turned the handle and passed through it.

Chapter 24

Vaughn and Jimmy left Garrity's house, running through the snow all the way back to the pickup. Neither spoke along the way as nothing needed to be said.

Jimmy had to remind Vaughn to slow down while he drove as the drifts and ice were treacherous. It was an agonizingly slow drive out to the campsite at Wellington Lake. It took over an hour. There was nothing to be done about quickening the pace. Vaughn raged and vented and slammed the heel of his hand down on his steering wheel in helpless protest. Vaughn cursed. His fingers squeezed the steering wheel.

Marzan's phone signaled an incoming text message as they passed through the ghost town of Pine.

"0-391-891-0533"

The numbers were map coordinates masquerading as a phone number. It was a rendezvous point. The coordinates were close, less than ten miles away.

Captain Rick had finally found him, gathering up his flock as any good shepherd would. It was likely that an escort would be waiting for him, there. Some earlier defector from Marzan's platoon must have learned about Jimmy going AWOL. *The insurgents have operatives inside the DSF*, he thought.

Marzan was a soldier and there was much work to do in defense of his country. A soldier must never confuse defending his country with defending the government. They are not the same.

"It's taking too god damn long," Vaughn shouted, as he slammed the dashboard again.

Jimmy calmed him again, reminding him to breathe and to focus. They could not risk any more speed.

They turned down an old Forest Service road that tracked back towards the lake. Vaughn knew the way to the campsite where Jessica was kept. "Why didn't I look there before," he asked. "It's so obvious."

"There's no way you could have known," Jimmy replied. "There have to be hundreds of campsites and scores of buildings out here. She could have been in any one of them or in none of them at all."

They followed the road down into a gulch filled with deep snow. Tire tracks were already laid there, probably by the kidnapper's truck that Vaughn saw at the Mercantile Building. Vaughn stayed in the tracks the best he could. He was rigid, grinding his teeth and breathing heavily. He pressed down on the accelerator and the tires spun out, pitching the back end of the truck to the right, precariously close to the edge which dropped some twenty feet down into a frozen creek bed.

"If we wreck, we'll have to walk out...if we can still walk," Marzan said. "I know how to survive in the cold but you and Jessica would probably freeze to death. So please slow down," Jimmy asked.

Vaughn straightened the truck out. One more bend in the road and a drop descending into the spruce trees and then down onto the plane of the creek. "There it is. Dead ahead!" Vaughn shouted. The campsite was marked by tire tracks. The snow was almost two feet deep. Old footprints dotted a pathway to an outhouse.

Vaughn jumped out with Jimmy close behind. "Jessica! Jessica!" he shouted.

Nothing.

He ran up to the steel door. It was padlocked. "Jessica!"

"Hang on," Jimmy said. He ran back to the truck and rummaged around in the cab.

"Jessica! Can you hear me?" Vaughn shouted. "Jessica! It's me!"

Jimmy returned with a tire iron and pried the latch loose with one jolt. Vaughn threw open the door and stormed in. It was empty inside. It had never been used, just like Garrity said. But Jess wasn't there. Vaughn lunged towards the seat and lifted the lid to look down into it. It was pitch black. Jimmy ran back to the truck.

"Jessica! Are you down there?" Vaughn shouted into the vault.

Jimmy returned with a flashlight and handed it to Vaughn. Vaughn shined it down the hole.

The flashlight was nearly dead. It was still too dark to see anything with its fading light.

Jimmy yanked on the crate that formed a bench seat for the toilet. The entire box came loose and slid away from the wall. Jimmy helped him push it out the door. Vaughn shined the light down into the opening again.

Nothing.

The opening was big enough for a man to climb down into.

"Have you got any rope in the truck?" Marzan asked.

"Yes. There's a tow rope in the box in the bed."

"I'll get it. Hang on," Marzan ran back to the truck again and returned with a rope. He tied one end around his waist and dropped the other end in the. "Go."

Vaughn took hold and climbed down. "Jessica!" He shouted as he descended.

The concrete pit was new. It was dry and clean and fairly warm. Jimmy went down about ten feet before touching the floor. He shined the dim flashlight around. "There are blankets!" A pile of blankets were piled over something. He kicked over a small propane heater as rushed to paw through them. "Jess!" He flung them aside. He found a hand. It was cold. "No! No!" He pulled the remaining covers off and followed the hand up a cold arm and up to a shoulder. He shined the flashlight on the face. It was her. It was Jessica. "I found her," he shouted up to Jimmy. She looked pale in the dim light. He touched her neck and her cheek. She didn't move.

"Jessica!"

He held her close to him in that dark, wretched place. He rocked her back and forth. "Am I too late?" He listened to her chest but didn't hear anything.

He shined the light in her face again. A faint mist floated up through the light. She was breathing.

"Jimmy, she's alive," Vaughn shouted, triumphantly. "Jess, can you hear me?"

Her eyes rolled under her eyelids.

"Jess! It's me."

She moaned.

"Tie the rope around her, under her shoulders. Then push her up to me," Jimmy shouted.

Vaughn looped the rope around her and lifted her up towards the opening. They got her out. Marzan threw the rope back down and Vaughn climbed out. They carried her to the truck and buckled her into the passenger seat. Jimmy reached in and turned the truck's heat all the way up. "You've got to get her to some place warm right away," Jimmy said.

Vaughn wiped tears out of his eyes with his coat sleeve. He smiled awkwardly and walked to the driver's side. But he noticed that Jimmy wasn't getting in. He was gathering up his things instead.

"We should get going," Vaughn said.

Jimmy Marzan grinned. "I'm not going back with you."

"Your commander?"

"Yes. I just got the message."

"It's freezing out here."

"I'll be all right. My unit's close. I can reach them by noon so long as I can stay hidden."

"Let me drive you to them," Vaughn offered.

"You can't get there by road. You'll just draw attention anyway. And you've got to get her in front of a good fireplace or something. She's probably dehydrated, too."

"I don't know what to say then, Jimmy. Thank you. Thank you for helping me. I'll never forget this."

"Just get her some place warm."

"I don't know how I can ever repay you."

"Don't worry about it."

Marzan slapped the fender with his hand, turned, and disappeared into the woods and darkness. Vaughn wiped the tears out of his eyes again, got into his truck, and headed towards home.

Jessica started to come around by the heat of the truck. She was mumbling incoherently. Vaughn had to get her down the hill to a hospital. That meant driving into Denver, after curfew.

When he finally reached U.S. 285, he pressed the accelerator, pushing his nerves to their limit on the winding, ice-covered highway. There were no other cars on the road, not even the government rigs with the blue eagles emblazoned on their trailers. It was as if the road had been closed to everyone except him.

"Jess, can you hear me?"

Jessica groaned but she had yet to open her eyes.

The snow was falling again and Vaughn clicked on his wipers to sweep the flakes away. The road was lit by an occasional highway streetlamp but three out of four were either turned off or burned out.

Vaughn checked the rearview mirror. There were headlights following him. The road dropped into a valley, crossed an intersection, and then came to a quarry known as Shaffers Crossing. The road blasted a steep ascent from there, up through a granite mountainside.

Vaughn checked his mirror again and saw that the lights were gaining. He scanned up the road to the glow of the next working street lamp, about a quarter mile ahead. The snow danced about in his headlights. He checked the mirror again. The vehicle was closing rapidly. Whatever it was, it was doing about sixty miles per hour which was insanity for the conditions. It wasn't a semi, it was too small.

He was on a more even section of the road now, close to the point where it split off into a divided highway. He pressed down on the accelerator. Vaughn aimed ahead to the next streetlamp, far up ahead. Suddenly, he saw vehicles in the middle of the road blocking the highway. He slowed and came to a stop in the four-lane road. Four military trucks barred the way some two-hundred yards ahead.

What should I do? he thought, as his truck idled.

The snow fell. The nearby streetlamp flickered. He checked his mirror. Back a few hundred yards behind, the truck that was following him had pulled off the highway onto the shoulder. Ahead, the black armored vehicles barred the way.

Jessica mumbled at his side.

The snowflakes flickered in the high beams.

Vaughn scanned the vehicles ahead. They were MRAPS, painted flat black. Vaughn had never seen military vehicles painted that color before. They had always been khaki or gray.

The truck behind pulled back out onto the road. He could see it was a county sheriff deputy's vehicle as its white broadside appeared for an instant before finishing its U-turn and going back down the highway the other direction.

The black MRAPS were still.

Vaughn's heart began to pound.

Jessica mumbled again and raised her arm to her forehead.

The deputy's truck disappeared completely from view.

Vaughn couldn't understand why no soldiers were hailing him or approaching. Something wasn't right.

What do I do? he thought.

"Vaughn..."

Jessica was coming to. She was struggling to open her eyes. He placed his hand behind her neck. He had to get her to a hospital. He pressed the accelerator and started forward, hoping the sentries would let him pass. He leaned in towards Jessica to whisper into her ear....

...But a flicker of light flashed ahead and not a fraction of a second after that he heard a dozen zips of bullets slicing the air. He slammed on the brakes. For a brief moment, Vaughn thought he should get out and throw his hands up in the air, but his better instincts took over. He slammed the transmission into reverse and stomped his foot down on the gas. The Ford roared to life, wheels spinning as it searched for traction. The treads grabbed hold and she barreled backwards down the highway. Vaughn pushed Jessica's face down onto the console with his right hand and looked back over his right shoulder to drive. Several thuds punctured the cab. The radio lit up and buzzed at full volume. The windshield fractured and shards of plastic and glass shrapnel exploded everywhere. One of the headlights blew out. Hot antifreeze splashed him in the face and its sweet, vomit-smell filled the cab.

He backed the truck at whining, full speed for about an eighth of a mile before executing a backing spin-out that would have rolled the truck eleven out of ten tries in any other circumstance, but his rig executed the maneuver perfectly. He stomped on the gas again and tore back down the highway towards Shaffers Crossing.

Vaughn glanced at his rearview mirror but the mirror was gone. The side mirrors were shattered as well. He didn't want to see what was behind him, anyway. Sometimes, you don't want to know what's gaining on you.

Jessica groaned. He felt her neck. It was warm and wet. He jerked his fingertips up to his nose and smelled it. It was sweet…just antifreeze, not blood.

The Ford was mortally wounded but she stammered, pinged, and rattled on for about a mile before decelerating and dying on the side of the highway.

Vaughn turned on the interior light. He checked Jessica. She wasn't bleeding. Her eyes were wide open. The radio buzzed on at full volume. Vaughn fiddled with the knobs to no avail. He turned the key to shut off the power to kill the ear piercing wail. He took a moment to catch his breath. It was so hard to breathe.

"Can you speak?" he asked her.

She nodded.

"Are you hurt?" he asked her.

"No. Are you?"

He was.

It was as if someone had swung and hit him with a heavy pipe just below the ribs. He knew it the instant it happened because he perceived a white flash. It was like seeing stars after getting hit in the head. A terrible pain worked its way down his left arm so that he could no longer move it. His adrenaline was wearing off. It was getting more difficult to catch his breath. He reached into his coat with his right hand and felt for the wound in his gut, a tear in the flesh just below his ribs. Warm fluid cascaded out of it. He didn't dare remove his hand because he didn't want Jess to see all the blood. "Vaughn," she asked, sensing something.

"I'm okay," he answered.

"Vaughn, are you hurt?"

"I'm..."

It was difficult for him to speak. He tried to catch his breath again.

Jessica reached her hand into Vaughn's coat and placed her hand on his. She put pressure on it but the more pressure they applied, the more the blood seemed to leak out between their fingers.

Jessica's eyes filled up.

"What do I do, Vaughn?"

"You go to my Mom's."

He trailed off. He couldn't get enough air in to speak anymore.

Jessica pulled close in to him. Her soft, golden hair, dimly lit by the dying glow of the lone streetlamp, fell down and caressed him. She held him, pouring her love into his wounded body.

They sat there in silence for some time.

Vaughn's breathing became erratic. His left arm was paralyzed. But he felt a presence flowing into him through Jessica's embrace, taking away his pain.

She pulled herself up and looked into his eyes. The streetlight went out. A bright white light filled the sky from the east behind them. Its glow illuminated all. It lit Jessica's face for a brief second, which amounted to an eternity of time in Vaughn's fleeting moments. In that instant, as he looked at her, he knew that everything would be all right. Jessica would live. She would be a mother again. He felt the completeness of his total love for her like an irresistible force. But he felt regret in that instant too. He regretted he would not be able to see his young daughter again. He thought of little Brooke and how much he just wanted to be able to be sipping imaginary tea and eating invisible crumpets with her — one last, priceless tea party.

He envisioned Brooke as a grown woman, strong and beautiful and proud and with a child of her own. He could see all of time now, as if he was there. He knew it would be so, as if he was remembering it — remembering a certain future.

He accepted his death. Everyone has to die, but not everyone lives. And few go out of this life wrapped in the embrace of the ones they love. Everything was going to be all right.

The white glow of plasma faded to black.

Jessica held Vaughn there in the darkness. She held him until the warmth began to leave his body. The Deputy Pritchard, the one who had given Vaughn the gas that one frozen night near the Mercantile Building, pulled around behind them. He told Jessica that he had desperately tried to catch up to them as they were hurtling toward the checkpoint. But he just couldn't make it in time. He had to turn back and shut down his vehicle before the radio-flash from the electro-magnetic pulse destroyed it.

Pritchard helped Jessica pull Vaughn's bloody body out of his tattered truck. His still warm blood spilled out of his body, melting into the snow beneath him. They loaded him into the back of the deputy's SUV. He drove them down the hill to Denver by the back roads, all the way to Vaughn's mother's house where Jessica was reunited with her daughter.

Chapter 25

Plan B was the only option, or so the president was convinced. Revolution was spreading across the western states like an August wildfire. Resistance metastasized as cells found each other, linked up, exchanged information, traded materiel, and coordinated plans of attack. It was getting beyond the capacity of the D.C. establishment to control. And if there's one thing any rotting establishment hates, it is losing control. There have never been any limits on what established orders will do to maintain their power. Things never change.

The collateral damage inflicted by the Domestic Security Force was captured in video and sporadically broadcast out to the rest of the world. Images of tanks and armored personal carriers rolling through Beaver Cleaver neighborhoods, demolishing cars and houses along their route, and troops in black storm trooper gear, kicking in doors were spreading virally.

The anxiety in the ranks of the establishment was turning into psychosis. The Department of Homeland Security finally succumbed to throwing the full internet kill switch to shut down the flow of information. The president was authorized to enact the security measure in an amendment to an earlier military spending bill so that Congress would go along. The establishment managed to regain control of information, for a whopping twelve hours, but a spontaneous order of thousands of computer hackers launched assaults on the government and their corporate shills, blowing their firewalls apart with routines loaded onto memory sticks and infecting and destroying the servers of their corporate collaborators. The virtual insurgents erased everything and replaced the output with a scrolling "V".

The truth was rerouted over landlines and radios and peer-to-peer internet. The pictures of the burned, and the bloated, and the sounds of rage and grief flowed again, blowing through the establishment's filters and censors. No tyranny can maintain control without lies; the truth is anathema to tyranny. The Gordian Knot of censorship that held the paradigm aloft was simply hacked through by the purveyors of truth. The edifice of the overlords came crashing down.

China condemned America's heavy handed response before the

U.N. Then Russia followed suit. Then even Iran piled on.

"Stay out of our affairs," snapped the president's Grand Vizier, otherwise known as the secretary of State. "The United States is a sovereign nation and has the right and...and more importantly, an humanitarian obligation to restore peace and security. We reserve the right to maintain order by whatever means is necessary."

Washington D.C. stood nearly alone, wobbling, supported internationally by only the U.K. on one arm and Israel on the other. The Prime Minister affirmed the United Kingdom's support of their "special friend" and their vicious deployment of "whatever means necessary" to preserve Anglo-Saxon hegemony. Israel, growing increasingly isolated, simply reminded their baying-wolf Arab neighbors that they were quite willing to use their nukes to defend themselves if necessary. Canada and Mexico pulled away and soldiered up their borders.

A million people demonstrated in D.C. in the weeks following the Civic Center Park Massacre. But MRAPS and phalanx after phalanx of storm troopers in black body armor and shields marched in and dispersed them. This worked against the state as the big, visible, containable demonstrations were diffused into millions of small, ones. The protests became ubiquitous.

The American implosion spread worldwide, emboldening partisans and insurgents in the farthest corners of the rapidly disintegrating empire. The ranks of the jihadists swelled. Already dangerously undermanned as troops were siphoned off to restore order in the U.S., American supply convoys were ruthlessly attacked. Airbases were overrun. Remote units were cut off from food and water and ammunition. A division-strength U.S. base in Shariastan was encircled and forced to surrender. It was the worst U.S. military defeat in sixty years. The Army colonel gallantly offered his life in exchange for giving quarter to his men. The fanatics were all too happy to oblige, beheading him and transmitting the video gore throughout the world.

The empire was finished.

The humiliated president never left Air Force One. His plane flew in continent-sized figure eights for four days at a time, flanked by fighters and refueling midair. He ruled in absentia, like one of those deposed, tin-pot despots. Things never change.

What will my legacy be? the president wondered. *Will I be remembered as the Nero who lost the republic?* The thought of the unsavory judgment by posterity crippled his reason. He decided he had to save the establishment at all costs.

He prayed.

He envisioned the first Savior of the Republic, the grim, log cabin messiah from Illinois with his stove pipe hat and his sunken jowls. In his vision, his hero reached down from the heavens and placed his boney hand on the contemporary president's shoulder. "Give me your wisdom, Abraham," the president prayed. The wisdom came to him like a bullet to the back of the head. From there, it was presented to a hastily arranged Cabinet meeting of his yes-men.

America's second Civil War was not going according to the 1861 playbook. There were no regulars to confront and subdue with supreme military force. There were no battalions of men in gray wool, aligning themselves in files to be annihilated with cavalry charges, firing lines, and Gatling guns. The modern revolution was everywhere, simultaneous, yet faceless. Civil disobedience froze the transportation systems and choked off the highways. Rebels launched shoulder-fired missiles at paramilitary helicopters. "Where did they get them?" the president demanded to know. "Those evil Chinese," his yes-men answered. Banker computer systems were hacked and the bank accounts of executives, running things from Costa Rica, were drained only to be replenished the very next day by Treasury Department keystroke entry. The prisons erupted. Communities began arranging their own security and black markets.

The D.C. establishment, embodied in human form by the god-pharaoh president, had one last desperate plan to restore the order. Plan B—The Sherman Doctrine. The citizenry had to be shocked-and-awed into submission. When the attorney general of Colorado—the highest-ranking elected officeholder remaining in the state—ordered all Colorado National Guards to return home to defend the state. That rebellious act was all the pretext that the president needed to implement his Plan B.

It was a small neutron bomb by military standards. The one used against Iraq's Revolutionary Guard was much more potent. This one was detonated extremely low in the air so as to minimize and contain the arc of the electromagnetic pulse. The tactical intent of the induced electronic blackout was to stifle the flow of information out of Denver and to incapacitate the resistance. Collateral damage was unfortunate, but utterly necessary in lieu of the dire circumstances. "Think of how many lives that will be saved in the long run," rationalized the president. "It is worth it. The republic must be saved."

The bomb achieved its goal with the radio-flash instantly frying the circuitry of anything receiving a current or not grounded. All the running automobiles stalled with their electronics cooked. A half-million cars would never start again. All the streetlamps went dark. Home computers and televisions and phones and radios went off. The power surge melted a good portion of the grid. Electricity was gone. In an instant, it truly had become 1864 for Denver. Denver became the new Atlanta after the vainglorious Sherman punitively burned it to the ground. The message was sent loud and clear to the rest of the country and to the world: Respect Washington's authority. Resistance is futile.

Fires raged for days after as there was no water pressure to put them out. Vaughn's mother kept watch over the night from her window as the twenty-foot flames engulfed a nearby school. The fire trucks just roared past it, their eerie sirens descending into the smoke. They had other destinations and other things to save that night.

Something told Vaughn's mother that it was time to go. She wiped her eyes for the last time and gathered Jessica and little Brooke. They headed north, walking right down the middle of the ten lanes of I25. There were only a handful of moving cars. The night sky was illuminated orange by the fires and permeated by the unseen roar of fighter jets and the thumping of helicopters above and the smell of gasoline and burning plastic. Vaughn's family was not alone on the road. The refugees marched in clusters of a dozen or so, thousands and thousands of silent figures moving north in the night, escaping a city on fire.

They walked ten miles away from the glow of the fire. They walked until they reached Vaughn's father's house. He took them in. They boiled potatoes and sugar beets on a grill in his backyard. It was the longest night of their lives until the next one, and then the next one after that. But they survived.

On the morning of the third day, a mechanized patrol left Camp Anubis. Their orders were to liberate the Jefferson County police substation in Evergreen. It had been taken over from the feds by local deputies.

The mechanized unit worked its way down Santa Fe Boulevard, directly under the neutron carnage, once known as Englewood. Their Geiger counters crackled as they motored through the stalled autos and the burned warehouses and past a derailed commuter train resting on its side, iron rails curled up like Christmas ribbons beneath it. A heavy cloud of soot blanketed the sky and occasional snowflakes — or were they ashes? — floated down as they advanced in that cold morning. The column of eight vehicles turned onto Hampden Avenue and rolled west.

Many of the soldiers were new recruits, filling the cavernous void left by the defections. They were given assurances that the radiation levels were benign but they were inoculated, just to be safe, with doses of Antirad. Never mind the side effects or if it even worked at all. Big pharma made a fortune on the contract. Even if the place was toxically radioactive and the Antirad was really just a trillion dollar placebo, the remaining soldiers of the Domestic Security Force were prepared to follow orders. The urban Hampden Avenue transformed into the mountainous U.S. 285. The patrol lumbered upward into the wooded foothills. They had to take a circuitous route as intelligence reports indicated that the road up through Idledale had sloughed off in an avalanche and was impassable. They turned off onto a winding two-lane road and continued their advance. The convoy's diesels rumbled slowly around the snaking, narrow road while the hillside walls steepened on either side.

The master sergeant cursed the other drivers when they bunched up. "God damn idiots!" he screamed into his radio.

The lieutenant rolled his eyes.

The sergeant urged the young lieutenant to reconsider the route. They could loop around one of the tendril roads, head back out to the highway, and come back in on county road 73 which was not so snaking and canyon-like. The know-it-all lieutenant refused. Military intelligence had warned that CR 73 might have IEDs.

Not considering what you don't know is chronic in youth. Young, arrogant officers refusing to heed the knowledge of their seasoned NCOs is nothing new. Things never change.

The lead Humvee stopped as it wound around a bend. The convoy coiled up behind it, sending the sergeant into a rage. The way was blocked on the narrow road by a three-car wreck. Perhaps they had collided a moment after the radio-flash had seized their engines and locked up their brakes. The armored DSF vehicles idled under the enfolding ponderosa pines and the overcast skies on the narrow canyon road. A cold breeze blew through the treetops.

A DSF soldier, designated point man, dressed in freshly procured black camouflage and gas mask, exited the first Humvee and approached one of the cars. He found a driver slumped over the wheel.

He reached in, grabbed him by the hair, and pulled him upright. The man's face was pale but recognizable. *He looks like that actor guy,* he thought. *What's his name? McDouglas?*

A glimmer caught his eye. It came from McDouglas's wrist. The soldier reached down and pulled off a shiny watch. "Movado!" he exclaimed. "Very nice." He tucked it into his breast pocket.

But a sense of uneasiness shot through him as he stepped back from the car. Something was out of place. *What's wrong, here?* he asked himself. He drew his rifle and scanned the trees through his scope. The branches swayed gently in the wind. Nothing. No movement. No shiny reflections. No geometric shadows. He looked up into the featureless gray heavens. He watched a black raven fly overhead and disappear behind the tree tops. There would be no air cover, today. Too cloudy. Flakes of ash — or was it snow? — fell down.

He scanned the cars. *The cars! That's it!* The car before him was the only one with a driver in it. That seemed unusual. *Maybe the others were too hurt to help the poor bastard out,* he thought. He checked the crumple zones of the wrecks. The damages did not align with their collision points. *It's not a collision. The cars were staged.* He shouted into his radio. "Something's wrong! We need to get turned around, stat!" He started back towards his truck, lumbering in all the radioactive mitigation gear he was wearing. He expected the zips of bullets or explosions at any moment. He caught a glimpse of a shadow within the shadows of the trees. There was motion in the woods. "Turn around! Turn around!" he shouted. "Get the fuck out of here!"

There was no room to turn around to escape. The caravan would have to back up. The trucks lurched into reverse. Their bunching up, a function of the arrogance of leadership and lack of experience, made the maneuver a complete snafu. The rear Humvee tried to back into the nearest turnout and whip around but this jammed all the other vehicles up waiting for him. The sergeant hopped out and started flailing about in an effort to coordinate the retreat. The point man hopped back into his vehicle. He yanked off his gas mask and pointed his rifle out the window.

"Get ready," he informed the driver.

"For what?" asked the rookie driver. "There ain't no one out here with the balls to attack us."

The rear Humvee whined as it backed a full fifty yards into the next turnout. It grind-shifted into drive just when the first IED went off, knocking it ten feet up into the air. Fireballs blasted out from its windows as it flipped rear over front, landing on its top, blocking the escape route for the others. The remaining seven trucks were trapped and a turkey shoot ensued. The trees came alive with muzzle flash. Bullets and rocket propelled grenades and white phosphorous reigned in on the convoy from the highpoints on either side. Within twenty seconds, all of the convoy's 50-caliber gunners were lost. The patrol's patrician lieutenant radioed frantically for air support. It would take fifteen minutes to get there and the cloud cover would make it a dicey operation at best. "We'll all be dead by then!" he screamed.

Five more IEDs exploded, knocking one more of the Humvees off the road and into the creek. The point man cajoled his terrified driver to step on the gas and run through the barricade of mangled cars. It was their only chance to survive, but the driver was paralyzed with fear. The point man grabbed the wheel and stomped on the gas himself. The truck lurched forward, then tore straight ahead into the wreckage where it bounced up into the air and onto the top of dead McDouglas's car. It almost made it over the top, but not quite. It was high-centered at a forty-five-degree angle, its four wheels spinning a hundred miles per hour with no surface to grip. Its doors were sealed shut by the wreckage.

In a panic, the four surviving DSF troops inside the stranded Humvee fired wildly outwards in all directions. If they could only hang on for a few moments—hang on until the air cavalry arrived. But it was not to be. A phosphorus grenade exploded on the cab and all the soldiers trapped inside were cooked into charcoal within seconds.

The ambush was over.

The victorious partisans came down out of the shadows of the trees to gather up what they could. A half dozen more shots rang out, signaling either euthanizing bullets or ammunition exploding in the intense heat of the fires.

Helicopters approached frantically from the east, chopping up the gray sky with their rotors.

"Move! Move!" shouted Captain Rick. "They're going to kill anything that moves in this canyon. Thirty seconds."

A dozen men in ponchos converged on the burning Humvees. They grabbed whatever was left of any use: cases of ammo, rifles, cans of diesel, tools. They efficiently stripped the Humvees and dead soldiers clean. Then they disappeared into the forest as the air cavalry closed in.

One of those partisan fighters was Jimmy Marzan, and something in the burning lead Humvee caught his eye. Several more rounds popped and clanged in the heat of the fires. The flames roared.

The sky thumped with the approaching gunships.

"C'mon, Marzan. Let's go!" barked his buddy.

But Jimmy had to take a closer look.

"The gunships are coming! Let's get out of here!"

Jimmy looked over the burning dead man riding shotgun in the lead Humvee. He stepped in close enough that he could feel the heat coming off him.

An exploded bullet zipped past him.

Marzan looked into the point man's charcoal face. It had split down the middle in the heat of the fire and it looked as though something had grabbed hold of its scalp from behind and pulled it back so taut that it had ripped away from the skull. Its eyes were soulless caverns. The nose had already burned off. The mouth was stretched open exposing a set of ivory horse teeth.

"C'mon, Jimmy! We've got to go!"

A ping of another exploded bullet rang out.

Jimmy could feel the sound of the approaching gunship rotors beating through his chest. They were close, but Jimmy remained. The eyeless wraith of the point man stared into Jimmy Marzan's soul. Jimmy stood firm, staring right back into the devil. He glanced down at the spectre's smoldering claw, still clutching his M4. There, Jimmy found the silver ring and the eye of Osiris.

Made in the USA
Charleston, SC
21 January 2014